ASSASSIN'S
CREED
FRAGMENTS
THE BLADE OF AIZU

T0025391

Also in the *Assassin's Creed – Fragments* series
and available from Titan Books:

The Highlands Children
(coming July 2023)

The Witches of the Moors
(coming Jan 2024)

The Blade of Aizu

Olivier Gay

TITAN BOOKS

Assassin's Creed – Fragments: The Blade of Aizu
Print edition ISBN: 9781803363547
E-book edition ISBN: 9781803363882

Published by Titan Books
A division of Titan Publishing Group Ltd
144 Southwark Street, London SE1 0UP
www.titanbooks.com

First edition: June 2023
1 3 5 7 9 10 8 6 4 2

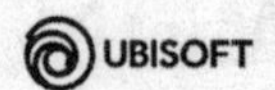

ORIGINALS

Map design by Darth Zazou.
Translation by Jessica Burton.

A CIP catalogue record for this title is available from the British Library.

Printed and bound in the United Kingdom by CPI Group (UK) Ltd, Croydon CR0 4YY.

1868

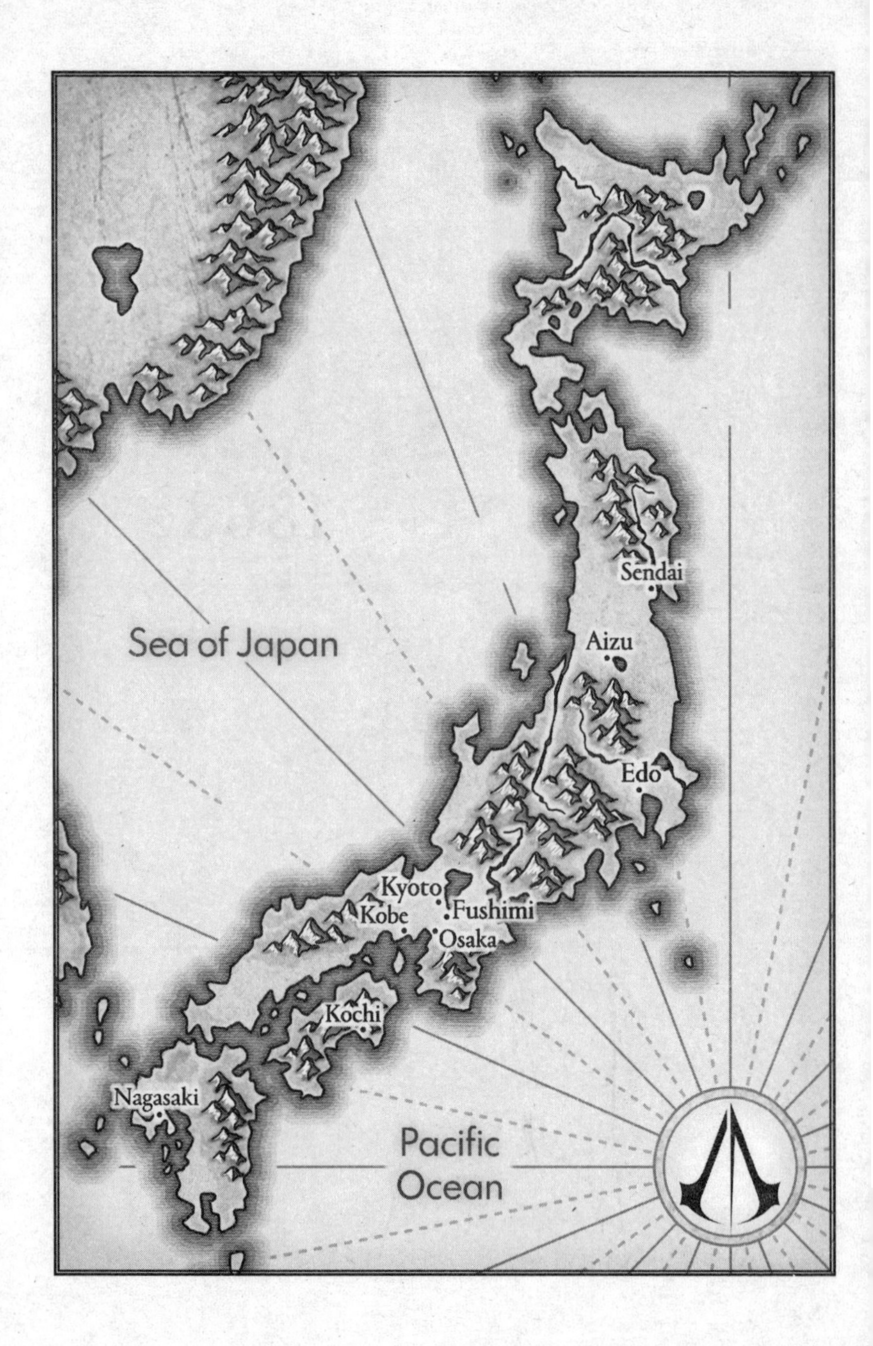
Sea of Japan
Sendai
Aizu
Edo
Kyoto
Fushimi
Kobe
Osaka
Kochi
Nagasaki
Pacific
Ocean

1

The two weapons clashed with a loud clunk and Atsuko stepped back, forced to cede ground. She had anticipated the move and pivoted on her right leg to return with a *tsuki*,[*] a low and long blow that should have hit her brother in the throat but slipped past him despite his defensive stance.

"This time, I'll…" she started.

She had no time to finish before he struck her sword faster than she had anticipated and she had to jump backwards to avoid being hit. She dove to the side, rolled over, and adopted a defensive position, just in time to avoid being spiked in her side by the *bokken*.[†] As soon as her shoulders hit the walls of the *dojo*,[‡] she knew he had manipulated her.

[*] Attack to the throat, with the aim of hitting the carotid artery.

[†] Japanese sword made of wood to imitate the shape of the katana, usually used for training.

[‡] Practice room for the learning of martial arts.

The weapon came towards her skull, she closed her eyes… and felt a gentle tap on her forehead.

"You talk too much," said Ibuka, dropping his guard.

Atsuko pushed aside the strand of hair that had fallen out of her bun and into her eyes, and stuck out her tongue.

"I hate you."

"'Course you don't. You love me."

"One doesn't prevent the other. I'll never beat you or even hit you. I'm no good."

The young girl slid to the floor in a sulk. After a moment's hesitation, her brother followed suit. His mischievous grin disappeared, replaced with a seriousness that seemed out of place for his age of seventeen.

"Don't say that. You're the most skilled girl I know."

"Yeah. The most skilled *girl*," she pouted.

"OK, OK. You're the most skilled *person* of sixteen I know. Hmm, or maybe the second; Hoshi is doing really well."

"But that's not enough to beat you."

Ibuka leaned against the wall, his hands behind his head, with an indolent expression like a Cheshire cat.

"Because I'm a genius, little sister. Everyone says so, so it must be true. It's not that you don't have talent; it's that I have too much."

"Oh, you're impossible," groaned Atsuko, punching him on the arm.

The worst thing was that he was right. Her brother was the golden boy of all the *samurai*[*] of Aizu, who had no hesitation in seeing him as the reincarnation of great legends of history like Miyamoto Musashi or Sasaki Kojiro. Everything Ibuka did seemed effortless: his blows were always precisely measured, his dodges perfect, his feints untouchable. He possessed phenomenal agility, stupefying reflexes, impressive coordination, and an intuition that was almost mystical.

In short, he was infuriating.

"One day I'll beat you," she promised quietly. "One day you'll make a mistake and I'll breach your defenses."

"One day, but not right now, little sister." He laughed as he ruffled her hair. "That being said, I was serious when I said how skilled you are. You're the one who's come closest. You almost put me in danger just now."

"Really?" gasped Atsuko, full of hope.

"No, not really, but I thought it might make you happy."

The teenage girl rolled her eyes. But it was difficult to stay mad at her brother for too long. He was so bright, always full of good humor. Plus, he had done so much for her.

After all, it was thanks to his support that she was allowed to train with weapons despite being a girl. When he realized

[*] Members of the warrior class who ruled feudal Japan from the beginning of the Edo era.

that she had been sneaking into the dojo to secretly do her exercises at the age of six, he had begged his father to let her join in his lessons. She had been able to learn not just *kenjutsu*,* but also *kyujutsu*,† *bajutsu*‡ and *jujutsu*§ at her brother's side and with the most eminent instructors of Aizu. Bless her father for permitting her such an enriched childhood.

As though the mere thought of him conjured his arrival, the stocky shadow of Shiba Tanomo appeared in the entry of the dojo. He was as massive as his children were skilled, with arms as big as a normal man's thighs and hands the size of anvils. But when he was not on the battlefield, he was the sweetest of men and the most tender of fathers.

"So who won?"

"You know very well," sulked Atsuko.

"But she did give me trouble," her brother gallantly defended her. "She has a real talent."

"Of course she has talent. She's my daughter." Tanomo gave them a huge smile. "I'm so proud of you both. Ibuka, you will become a great samurai, I'm sure of it. Your adventures will spread throughout Japan and will even reach the ears of the Emperor of Edo."

* Traditional Japanese sword art of the samurai.

† Traditional Japanese archery, practiced by samurai.

‡ Traditional Japanese art of war on horseback.

§ Art that brings together combat techniques developed by the samurai in the Edo era.

Despite the sincere compliment, the young girl was crushed.

Her father had not mentioned her on purpose. She may have been skilled with a *katana*[*]—less so than her brother for sure, but who could top him?—but she would never become a samurai. Tanomo had already proved his incredible open-mindedness in letting her train as a man. No doubt he had had to smile and endure the acidic remarks of his friends and their comparisons with their daughters.

She knew the majority of fathers expected their daughters to be well-presented, smiley, docile and ready for a good marriage, if possible into an influential family in the court. The samurai were respected, but their prestige was in decline and their fortunes were diminishing in the age of mercantile trade. More and more, the bourgeois were winning over the favor of the Emperor, and the warriors had little influence in times of peace. This trade-off worked perfectly between the commoners seeking respect and the depleted samurai.

Moreover, Atsuko was well aware that she had few friends. The girls her age did not share the same types of interests and didn't stop talking about boys. Oh, she had tried so hard to integrate. She had even gone to the effort of

[*] Sword of more than twenty-four inches, symbol of the samurai caste.

combing her hair and wearing a *furisode*[*] for the occasion of the *Setsuban*[†] just like all the other single girls in her town. The result had not been what she had hoped for.

Yasuhime had mocked the scar on the left side of her temple, the result of a misjudged dodge two weeks prior; Tomoe couldn't maintain her stern posture amidst the laughter of the other girls; and even though Munemi pretended to be more understanding than the others, it had only been to casually ask Atsuko if her brother was seeing anyone at the moment.

Yes, Atsuko's father was incredible; but even he could not go against tradition. Long ago, female samurai existed and were even particularly well respected. But that era was definitively over.

Which, she concluded petulantly in her head, wasn't fair at all.

"You didn't come here simply to compliment us," stated Ibuka, seeking out his father's gaze. "What's the real reason for your visit?"

Tanomo boomed with laughter as big as his shoulders, just as huge as his arms.

"So I can't keep even the slightest secret from you? Very well. We have been invited to Matsudaira Katamori's house

[*] Type of kimono, and the most noble traditional Japanese wear.

[†] Japanese national festival celebrating the arrival of Spring according to the ancient lunar calendar. Today, it is celebrated on February 3 each year.

in a week. He has heard about your exploits and wishes to meet you. I don't want to give false hope, but it's possible he's looking for new *hatamoto*."*

Ibuka leapt to his feet, and in his excitement, dropped his bokken onto his bare toes.

"*Ow!*" he cried, blushing right up to his hairline.

"That's exactly the type of behavior that must be avoided during the feast." Tanomo chuckled. "Our *daimyo*† is expecting a young man of legend, a new Musashi, and not a teenager gone to seed who cannot control his emotions."

Despite his cordial tone, Atsuko could detect an undercurrent of worry. Her father was not at ease in the high society of Aizu; one did not refuse an invitation from their daimyo, but he would probably spend the week ruminating and worrying about what could go wrong and potentially bring dishonor on the family. Tanomo was a fearless warrior, proven by all the scars on his chest—and none on his back, he would insist proudly—but he knew that his bear-like manners did not make him popular at ceremonies and official dinners. His son had the opportunity to make a good

* Official guard of a daimyo or Shogun (master), in feudal Japan. The hatamoto were often used as an elite force or rapid reinforcement in the direct service of the Tokugawa shogunate.

† Japanese title for a noble, which means a master, a governor from the military class, who acted under the orders of the Shogun in feudal Japan.

impression, and perhaps there would not be another.

"I will do my best not to embarrass you, Father," replied Ibuka, rubbing his big toe.

"I am certain of it. Atsuko, you are invited too, of course."

The teenage girl looked at her father, her mouth wide open. Was she dreaming?

Had she been mistaken from the beginning about his intentions? Was he really ready to defy tradition? Could she too be chosen to protect the daimyo? After all, if anyone could bring a woman into his personal guard, it would be Matsudaira Katamori. No one would ever question his decisions.

"Really?" she whispered, ready to cry.

"Of course," confirmed her father, smiling at her tenderly. "It will be the chance to bring out that magnificent furisode you wore to the festival. You wouldn't believe the number of compliments it brought you. Whatever you might think, you're a very attractive girl when you make a bit of effort."

Atsuko felt her heart break. Suddenly, she could hardly breathe.

"What do you mean?" she barely managed to spit out.

"Dad, you're so tactless," protested Ibuka. "Atsuko looks incredible even when she doesn't make an effort."

"Ah, right, of course! I'm sorry, you know me, I've never been good at finding the right words," apologized Tanomo, with another fit of laughter. "All I meant was that you looked wonderful in your dress, and that I'm sure you'll make just as big of an impression as your brother at the daimyo's reception."

But not for the same reasons, thought the young girl sulkily.

Her father was full of good intentions but had no idea how much his words wounded her. The blessed period of her life was most certainly over. Even though she had followed the exact same training as her brother, their paths were about to separate. He would become a samurai while she would marry some Imperial paper-pusher who had the good sense to find her appealing in a *kimono*.

Now was the moment to talk to her father, right this second, now. She would never again have as much courage as she had in the dojo where she had spent so much of her life. She once again sought out the spark in his eyes, and was struck by inspiration and began:

"Father… I wanted to ask you—"

He turned towards her, so big, so gigantic, with his loving look and unfailing confidence in his children.

"Of course," he interrupted with a generous wave. "If you want a new dress, I can try to arrange it. You know we are not as rich as we were before, but nothing is too good for my daughter. How would you feel about going to see old Hanae tomorrow? They say she gets fabrics directly from the capital."

Atsuko tried to dry her eyes discreetly on the sleeve of her training tunic. A good daughter of a good family did not cry in public.

"Of course," she sniffed. "I would love that."

2

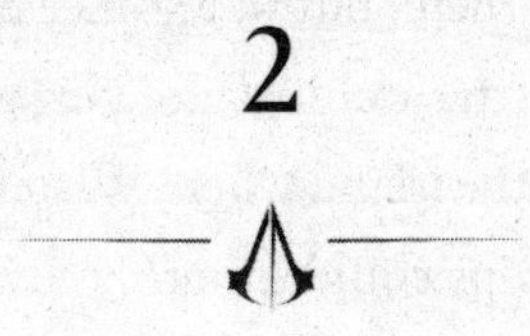

Summer in Edo could be stifling. It had not rained in two months and the city baked under the scorching sun. The daimyo families could shelter under the shade of the trees in their large gardens around the castle, but the commoners could not afford the same luxury. The cherry trees that adorned the Imperial route dropped their branches during the heatwave and the merchants had moved their carts to the Buddhist temples to benefit from the shade of the frontispieces. As soon as they could, the residents flocked to refresh themselves on the banks of the river Sumida, sometimes forgetting that they did not know how to swim, and the treacherous waters had already claimed several careless people.

Under the heavy atmosphere, tempers were quick to flare, and despite the efforts of the guards, crime rates had never been so high. Tavern disputes often ended in deaths or injuries, so much so that the bodies of the losers were found abandoned on the streets.

Edo was the capital of the Empire, the center of cultural, political, and economic life in Japan. However, the situation would not worsen there, but in another more modest town at the other end of the archipelago, Nagasaki. It was one of the only places on the island where Westerners were allowed and where their ships could moor.

That night, two British sailors disembarked and headed for the downtown area to enjoy the pleasure sector. They had spent several months at sea, had full pockets, and expected to fully enjoy their night.

They were found dead the next day.

And the destiny of Japan was shaped.

"You can't let this go! If you say nothing, the situation will repeat itself and the British Empire will become the laughingstock of the world!" gasped William Lloyd.

In one gulp, he emptied the glass the server had just brought him.

Lloyd loved tea, like every British person blessed to be so, but he could never get used to the ceremony arranged by the Japanese around it. Served quickly, drank quickly, that was how he liked his drink. That left him more time to attend to important affairs.

And this affair was *particularly* important.

In front of him, Harry Parkes lowered his gaze, unable to maintain his fiery glare. The British consul was an experienced and competent man, but he did not have the stomach to make difficult decisions. He remained convinced that a bad peace was worth more than a good war, and that the most efficient change was brought about slowly by extensive cooperation.

In short, he suffered from an incorrigible sense of idealism.

This was why the Order of the Templars had operated in the shadows to assign one of theirs to act as his right hand. In this prestigious post, Lloyd could follow the political cogs between the British Empire and the archipelago in real time.

And, sometimes, even influence the events—with or without the consent of the consul.

"Rest assured, I do not intend to remain inactive," concluded Parkes with a grimace. "I have already requested an audience with the Emperor to express my displeasure and that of the whole Commonwealth. I expect to carry out a thorough investigation in Nagasaki and ask to have the city put under curfew until we have found those responsible. And when we get our hands on them, justice will be swift. The residents must understand that we are untouchable."

Parkes clearly expected congratulations—after all, it was a pretty firm reaction—but Lloyd snorted in derision.

"Oh, an investigation? Fantastic, the murderers will be trembling in their boots. The questioning will lead to nothing, or they'll find some poor scapegoat to put to the sword to appease us. Might as well spit in our faces. Young men are dead, Harry. British citizens who we swore to protect. They were twenty-three years old, their whole lives ahead of them, and someone massacred them. What will other sailors think on their vessels, knowing that we barely lifted a finger? What will they think of us? It's this cowardice that..."

The consul furrowed his brow and Lloyd stopped himself in the middle of his tirade, conscious of pushing too far. Parkes was an excellent consul in the political sense, known throughout the world, and angering him would be counterproductive.

However, instead of reprimanding him, the consul fell into his armchair, his head lowered.

"I know," he sighed. "But my hands are tied. The *Shogun** Tokugawa is far too powerful and has no intention of helping us in our task. Look how fast he accepted French aid to modernize their army. He has clearly chosen his side—and it isn't ours. If we try to defy him directly, we will not necessarily come out the winners."

* Military chief who wielded the real power in feudal Japan, with the Emperor occupying a more honorific and traditional role.

Lloyd poured himself another glass of tea and grimaced while he took a swig. Parkes wasn't wrong. Emperor Mutsuhito was only fifteen years old and had but a ceremonial role. The real power belonged to the samurai, to the daimyos and to the most important of them all, the Shogun Tokugawa. Installed in the palace in Edo, he reigned as a monarch, and no one could go up against him. His alliance with France had only solidified his position.

The Templars in London had been very clear in their instructions. The institutions must be respected, the authority of the Emperor reinforced, so that the central power would allow for the implantation of the Order on the island.

And Tokugawa was a sizable object.

Lloyd subconsciously stroked the hilt of the katana he wore on his side. He was one of the only Westerners to have the privilege of carrying the curved sword. The weapon had been forged by the most famous blacksmith in the Imperial court, in recognition of his talent. In the twelve years he had lived in Edo, he had abandoned traditional European weapons to embrace the way of *budō** with the same brutal efficiency he brought to all situations. He had triumphed in countless duels and the courtesans murmured behind his back that he was not human, that he must

* Practice grouping all Japanese martial arts like karate, judo, etc.

have made a pact with an *oni*[*] to become so dangerous.

If only politics could be so easily resolved. If only he could defeat the Shogun in single combat. But no, it was only fantasy.

"We aren't in the best situation," he responded in a reasonable manner. "The Japanese are in the wrong. They should have protected our men while they were on land. That was one of the conventions we signed with them. We have the right to claim compensation. As Nagasaki depends on the Tokugawa clan, that would embarrass him in the face of the Emperor."

"And what would that do?"

"Maybe nothing. Maybe something. More than doing nothing, in any case. If we could create a schism between the Emperor and the Shogun, we could eventually benefit."

"The Emperor is fifteen," disagreed Parkes. "He would never dare to go against the Shogun."

"For the moment, no." Lloyd confirmed. "But he will grow up. I don't know if you remember your adolescence, Harry, but it's a time when you don't appreciate limits, or orders, or restrictions, or bullying. Maybe Mutsuhito will start to realize he is only a puppet Emperor. Maybe he ends up asking himself if the Shogun isn't a bit too powerful."

[*] Creatures of Japanese folklore, a sort of malicious spirit, a demon, comparable to a yokai.

"So? Even if that were the case? What could he do against the power of Tokugawa alone?"

Lloyd gave a sinister smile.

"Alone? He wouldn't be alone. Several clans don't appreciate the omnipotence of the shogunate and would be ready to support the Emperor. And I am certain that Her Gracious Majesty Queen Victoria would support the occupant of the throne against his usurper."

"You aren't suggesting—" gasped the consul.

Lloyd waved his hand over Parkes' worries.

"No, of course not. No one would come out a winner, except the blasted French. But the simple fact that we could imagine doing so would make even a megalomaniac like Tokugawa think twice about it. He knows he is in the wrong for not protecting our men. If he thinks we're ready to go to war to get compensation, he will no doubt do the honorable thing."

"And if he doesn't?"

"In that case, the Queen will know for sure who are allies of the Commonwealth and who are not."

Tokugawa stopped his pacing when he heard a knock on the door. He had insisted that he must not be disturbed, and the simple fact that the servants had let someone in showed it was someone important. He readjusted the folds of his kimono, took a few seconds to smooth the frown lines on his forehead and, satisfied, granted the visitor entry.

The man who entered the room walked with the grace of a warrior despite his fifty years. Numerous medals adorned his uniform, but he somehow managed the feat of walking without having them click. He moved like a shadow.

He could give lessons to some of our *shinobi*,* thought Tokugawa icily, before turning to look out of the window.

"*Capitaine* Brunet. I was expecting you earlier in the day. It is very late for a visit."

"I came as quickly as I could," apologized the man. "I was with your troops on the other side of Edo when your messenger contacted me. I can come back tomorrow, if you prefer?"

"No, stay, now that you're here. I suppose you are aware of the situation."

The captain nodded. He had lived in Edo for almost twenty years. He had been named to the post by Napoléon III to assist the Japanese army in modernization, and even though the French Emperor had long since abdicated, Brunet remained at his post. He knew the goings on of the city by heart, and few rumors escaped him.

* Traditional name given to ninjas, who form a certain category of spies and mercenaries.

"Two British sailors were killed in Nagasaki. The English are furious and believe that their protection was your responsibility. They demand compensation."

"Well summarized. Consul Parkes met with me at midday. He demands—demands!—the resignation of the governor of Nagasaki, and requests five hundred police be sent to protect the foreign sector. He would consider any refusal of these terms to be a declaration of war."

Brunet frowned. He knew Parkes well, a likable and sympathetic politician, and while he did not have the same objectives as Brunet, he always seemed to be reasonable and sought to gain British influence on the archipelago by any means. Such a demonstration of force wasn't like him; Japan was still demoralized from the terrible humiliation of the bombing at Shimonoseki.

"Don't back down," suggested Brunet. "The Brotherhood will support you discreetly, as always."

"The Brotherhood, eh?" repeated Tokugawa, disaffectedly. "A Western organization that has no influence on this island. In any case, why would it be concerned about what happens here?"

Brunet broke into a large grin.

"You are mistaken. Our influence is bigger than you could imagine—and we are here to help you."

"But, why? Don't tell me it's out of simple altruism."

"Let's say I like you a lot," continued Brunet. "Okay, that's not enough. So, let's say instead that the situation in Japan is fragile at the moment. Your Emperor is feeling caged-in by his honorific robes and position, and it is only a matter of months before he decides to take the real power. Your feudal organization does not appeal to him, and he considers that the daimyos and yourself, the Shogun, belong to the past. We do not agree. We believe that power belongs to the people, the peasants, the samurai, the regions—not to a faraway Emperor in his isolated palace."

Tokugawa took a moment to consider what his opposite was saying. He had tried to gather intel on the Assassins these last years—what general did not take the time to know his enemy?—but had found very little. What he did understand was that the Brotherhood had played a role throughout the history of Europe, whether through the Crusades or the French Revolution.

Powerful allies for sure, but were they trustworthy?

"That's not all," growled the Shogun. "The English were not content with just knocking at my door. They also went to see the Emperor directly. Of course, they told him their version of events, and Mutsuhito is convinced that I'm in the wrong and that I wasn't up to protecting guests on our land. He is pressuring me to accept the British demands and that I make a public apology."

This time, Brunet shook his head. While he had worked on excellent relations with the shogunate, the British had progressively succeeded in winning the ear of the Emperor. Any difference in opinion between the two would destabilize Japan. What were the English playing at?

"What will you do?"

"What do you think? I won't alienate myself from both the Emperor and the British in one swoop, especially because they have a legitimate reason to accuse me. I will accept the demands of the consul and swear to do everything in my power to find the murderer of the two British sailors."

"Aren't you afraid of what your daimyos will say? Some will take this as a sign of weakness. They'll think you won't hesitate to sacrifice the governor of Nagasaki in order to protect your own position."

Tokugawa clenched his fists and advanced towards Jules Brunet. The French captain was particularly large, and the Japanese man only reached up to his shoulder, but that didn't stop him crumbling under him.

"My daimyos obey me. Besides, they understand honor. They know that the English demand justice for their dead."

"Justice, yes," corrected Brunet softly. "But blind vengeance, that's not..."

He broke off mid-sentence and stared. Tokugawa opened his mouth to speak, but the captain put his fingers to his lips to dissuade him. Without warning Brunet leapt towards the large castle window that led to Edo Bay and pushed aside the curtain.

The moon was in its first quarter and barely illuminated the walls, but in the flickering candlelight, the Shogun thought he saw a shadowy figure, folded in on itself like a hideous gargoyle on the roof.

Brunet let go of the curtains and slipped his hand under his military doublet to draw a dagger with the fluidity of a movement repeated thousands of times. The blade struck in the direction of the intruder, who kicked out, and it missed by the slightest width. The captain leaned over the window ledge but could only stand and listen, powerless, to the scratch of steel against the walls. He wasn't stupid enough to believe that the stranger had succumbed to the fall. The shinobi were capable of the most impossible acrobatics and could find a hold on the smoothest surfaces. The rubble walls of the Tokugawa residence were like a blessing for them.

"What was that?" gasped the Shogun, who still hadn't moved an inch, even in his surprise. "Or rather, *who* was that? As assassin?"

"A spy," responded Brunet simply, stowing his weapon as though nothing out of the ordinary had happened. "Someone who absolutely needed to know what we were talking about, and what your decision would be over the two sailors."

"If he had wanted to kill me, he could have," observed Tokugawa, leaning over the threshold and looking up and down the court below. "Tens of guards, and not one of them capable of stopping the threat."

"I would have protected you, sir," stated the captain, gently bowing his head. "France could not permit the loss of one of its greatest supporters. Plus, I really do like you."

Still in shock, the Shogun gave a weak smile. At that moment, he did not feel like the most powerful man in the country, but more like a child, afraid of the dark and wondering whether the monsters under his bed were real. It wasn't the first time that Brunet spoke the truth; Tokugawa was a brilliant man and fine politician, but he was no soldier. He had no taste for combat or violence, which put him in a delicate position in directing the elite warrior class of the country.

"I must retire," said Brunet. "Should I ask the guards to come and secure your living quarters?"

"Yes," started the Shogun, before frowning. "No. I cannot show any weakness. Not now. I'll be okay with one bodyguard, and I'll sleep in my wife's bedroom for once. That will make her happy, for sure."

"I am sure, sir," confirmed Brunet diplomatically.

"But who could have sent a spy this way?"

"What do you think? I could never accuse them without proof, but I imagine the British were particularly interested in our reaction to their pressure strike."

"They would never dare. If the spy had been captured and denounced them, it would be war."

The captain shrugged his shoulders.

"Maybe that's what they want, after all. As you said, they seem especially aggressive at the moment. With that, sir, I'll leave you to sleep. I've already taken enough of your time."

He left the room, but before closing the door he added:

"Of course, if it did ever come to the worst, you should know that the Third Republic will be at your side—or at the very least the French forces already on the island will be."

"How reassuring," murmured Tokugawa.

But his gaze never left the ripped curtain lying on the floor, and the black night that threatened to engulf him.

3

Atsuko was far removed from the courtyard and the power struggles between the Assassins and the Templars. She could not stop replaying the conversation with her father and the way she'd been rejected without the slightest exception to her being a girl. As though all these years had never happened. She would get back in her place, back into the shell, and that was it. And the worst thing was that she couldn't even hold it against her father who, at the very least, had given her an incredible childhood. What he did, he did for her own good, she was sure of it.

It didn't make it any easier to accept.

"Hey, hurry up!" complained Ibuka. "I've been waiting for you for twenty minutes! We have a two-hour journey and I want to be back before sunset. Plus, I have no desire to get lost in the mountains… the sooner we leave, the sooner we'll be done."

Snapped out of her melancholic thoughts, Atsuko tried to put on a brave smile. Her brother was right: she was spending so much time ruminating that she was neglecting her duties. The situation wasn't Ibuka's fault. He hadn't asked to be born a boy, just like she hadn't chosen to be a girl.

"I'm coming!" she yelled, quickly tying up her hair in a bun.

Their father had purchased a prize cow from Kokan, the farmer who lived on the other side of the hills. It wasn't the closest farm, but he offered fair prices and never tried to lie about the quality of his beasts, which was more than could be said for most of the farmers of Aizu. However, his prices did not include delivery, and Tanomo had asked his two children to take care of the details, which involved a long trip over rocky terrain. The outward journey would be mostly okay because the sun that covered Edo in a heatwave was more bearable up here, but the return, guiding a cow by the neck, would be a real ordeal.

"We can't hold it against Father," insisted Ibuka. "He absolutely must offer the whole household a feast to celebrate the invitation from our daimyo. If you want to know what I think, he's putting the cart before the horse—or the cow, in this case. I'm not a hatamoto yet, and you're not married yet."

"No, right," replied Atsuko more tersely than she had intended. "But that's what he wants, and we won't disappoint him. If he wants a cow, then we bring him back a cow."

Ibuka looked at her with surprise. She had always seen him as a perceptive boy, but he was acting surprisingly immovable to her mood. Maybe he had always known what she was only just discovering: her lessons had only been an inoffensive pastime and not preparation for a life of combat.

No, she'd promised herself to stop thinking about it. It was a nice day, and she might as well enjoy the walk.

The two teenagers proceeded valiantly to the path that led up the hills. They were both in excellent physical condition and were walking at a good pace, until Ibuka proposed to spice things up.

"Race you to the second summit. Winner gets—er—the best cut of beef."

"Father decides our part," protested Atsuko.

"Not if we tell him about our bet. Don't tell me you're afraid to lose."

"No, it's just so childish—"

Before finishing her sentence, the young woman launched herself forwards, gaining three seconds over her brother.

"Hey that's cheating!" he yelled, before setting off in pursuit.

Ibuka ran with all his strength; his legs took on the ascents, ran down the descents. His sister bounded from rock to rock, livelier than a deer. No, not a deer, a majestic stag. In the dojo, she was neither as muscled nor as skilled as her brother. But her legs had nothing to stop her here, and she was free. Her heart beat hard in her chest, her lungs burned, but stopping or even slowing down was out of the question.

Her katana beat against her thighs and almost stabbed her twice. Her father insisted that his children always wore their swords. He explained that the region could be dangerous and that brigands sometimes roamed the area. But the real, more cunning, reason was that the weapon was an integral part of the samurai and its weight had to become as natural as wearing clothes. Normally, it didn't pose any problems, and Atsuko often forgot that she was carrying a weapon. That wasn't the case right now as it dangerously flapped at her thighs.

She felt that she was close and accepted the pain without even changing pace. Behind her, the ragged breathing of her brother spurred her on, gave her wings, let her transcend. The wind of the race made her cry, and through her tears she finally saw the summit. Her brother's steps neared dangerously, but in a fit of rage and willpower, she found a last reserve of energy and accelerated.

She surged in first place to the top of the hill and let herself fall to the ground, her arms crossed and out of breath. She counted in her head up to six before Ibuka appeared, exhausted and his legs dragging. He dropped next to her, struggling for breath. For a long moment, neither said a word, their eyes on the sky and waiting for their hearts to stop beating so hard.

"Six seconds," stated the teenage girl.

"Huh?"

"I cheated, I set off before you, so you lost a little time. But even so, you arrived six seconds after me. I won fair and square."

"Undisputedly," said her brother. "Honestly, I thought I'd catch you at the end, but you still had some energy reserves. Well done! It was really impressive."

Atsuko felt herself blush uncontrollably. She was proud of herself, far more than was warranted for a simple race.

She had overcome her limits. She had beaten her brother.

She rolled onto her side and got up gingerly, realizing too late that she had lay down on some wood, an imprint of which was now firmly embedded in her back.

She looked towards the farm with a lighter heart, as if she had proven something.

"Ah there you are finally!" grumbled the farmer as he saw them arrive. "I've been waiting for you for an hour!"

"We apologize, esteemed Kokan," said Ibuka bowing his head. "But we did run a large part of the way."

"It's not the speed that matters, but the moment you set off. If you had left at dawn, you would already be home by now. Anyway, no matter. Did your father give you the agreed amount?"

Atsuko took out the purse that her father had entrusted her with and handed it over to the seller, who examined the contents scrupulously before leading them to a prize cow, radiating good health with its shiny coat.

"This is one of my best animals," Kokan observed. "You can check in the stable if you like. Don't forget to tell Tanomo, so he knows that Kokan always keeps his word."

"I don't need to check," insisted Ibuka. "Everyone knows that your honesty is beyond compare. We would never have crossed the mountains if it were not so."

"Mm, well. Don't forget to mention it to your father all the same. I owe him a debt, and this cow is the start of paying him back. He'll know what I'm talking about."

The brother and sister looked at each other in surprise. Tanomo hadn't made any mention of a debt, but that was not so surprising. He rarely spoke about himself and even less about his past.

"May we know how our father helped you?" tried Atsuko.

"It's up to him to tell that story, if he wishes to," replied Kokan in a serious tone. "All that matters is that you're leaving with my prize cow. Take care of it. Its meat will be delicious."

Ibuka tried to lead the cow by its neck, but it moved slowly until he gave it a smack on the flank. The farmer watched them leave with a sorrowful look, like he was watching the best meal of the year walk away, before returning inside.

"What do you think Father did for him?" asked Atsuko,

burning with curiosity. "You think he saved his life during a war?"

"What war?" argued her brother. "These lands have been calm for years."

"For years, yes. But Kokan isn't exactly young. Maybe twenty years ago when Father was young..."

"It's hard to imagine Father as a young man." Ibuka laughed. "I bet he already had shoulders as big as ours combined."

"And hands as big as our heads!" replied his sister. "Luckily we take more after Mother."

"I wouldn't have minded getting a little of his strength. They say he could pull apart a horseshoe with his bare hands when he was young."

"Ah, don't believe every story you hear! He's strong, sure, but nobody could..."

"But just look at this magnificent beef! Even just looking at it I'm already drooling! So, lovers, did nobody warn you this road is dangerous?"

Atsuko turned sharply and found herself face to face with a boy of about twenty perched on a branch at the side of the road. He looked thin to the point of malnourishment, and wore a katana with a naked blade on his shoulder as if it were a peasant scythe. Atsuko had lived a sheltered life and never been in any real danger, but now her survival instinct was screaming that this person was dangerous.

Ibuka moved his hand to the hilt of his own katana. He was the model of calm and authority, and Atsuko felt her breathing calm. Of course. How could she worry? She was in no danger with him.

"Thanks for the warning. Luckily, we know how to defend ourselves against any dangers on the route. And plus," he decided to add, "we're brother and sister."

"Even better," said the stranger. "A brother, a sister and a cow. I can only imagine the incredible orgies. Now I know why you're heading for the hills, to escape the judgment of others."

His toothy smirk disappeared, and his expression darkened.

"Enough kidding around. Come out, everyone."

On his orders, four more men surged out of the bushes. They were all dressed as poorly as the first, though one of them had managed to find an oversized leather breastplate from some unknown battlefield and had patched it up with leather.

Two of them carried hatchets, while the third brandished a lance with a sharpened point and the fourth was twirling a *naginata** threateningly.

Atsuko felt adrenaline invade her. She unsheathed her katana and put herself back-to-back with her brother to try

* A type of curved scythe blade, often used for cutting off horses' legs on the battlefield.

and face the whole group. Their father had warned them about the brigands that lived on the edge of town and took advantage of travelers.

"So, they want to die," chortled the leader.

He ran his thumb along the edge of his blade to prove it was sharp, and drops of blood soon formed. He sucked his thumb without taking his eyes off his prey.

"It's a bit stupid to cut it like that just for show," observed Atsuko. "It could get infected."

"When I need a lesson in herbs, I'll ask for it, slut," said the man. "Right. You have the choice. You both seem brave, you're both wearing katanas, and I'm sure that the boy at least knows how to use it. So, you could decide to fight us. But let me warn you, that will end badly. There are more of us and we're more experienced. Real fights aren't like in the dojo, kids, and a katana is no bokken. If I hit you, you'll piss blood like a pig. So, what do you think, brats? Maybe I'll cut off your arm up to the elbow and let you live. Do you feel like spending your whole life an invalid? Or maybe I'll kill you slowly, cut by cut: I don't know. Let's find out."

"You don't scare us!" shrieked Atsuko in a trembling voice.

"Oh? But you must be worried. There are five of us and only two of you. I've killed twenty-seven people in the last two years. What about you? Do you think you're up to the challenge? Especially you, little girl? Even though you're the one worried about a wound that *could infect*?"

Atsuko's palms were soaking—she'd never sweated so much in training. She shifted her grip on her katana and inched closer to her brother. She suddenly couldn't breathe, and her bladder was burning.

"If not, there's always the chance you could just give us this nice fat cow and leave safe and sound. We're not so cruel, after all. We don't kill out of pleasure, just necessity. I'm a benevolent man. If you leave the cow, we won't even mug you. You can keep your katanas and your purses. Given the price of swords, you'd be the winners. Oh, and you, girly, I won't even rape you. Don't feel like it. So, you see, you can walk away well from this."

"What about us?" protested the brigand with the naginata.

"Yeah, what if we feel like it?" insisted the one with the lance.

"She'd fight harder for her virginity than for the cow," sighed the leader. "Let's be reasonable. I bet they already won't want to live with themselves after losing such a fine cow."

Atsuko's ears were ringing. And suddenly, she realized that her brother hadn't said anything for several minutes. That wasn't normal. He wasn't one to be shaken, no matter the situation. His confidence often came across as arrogance, and he could easily turn around any situation. With his talent for the katana, he could no doubt take these five brigands on his own. So why wasn't he reacting? Why wasn't he laughing in their faces? Why wasn't he reassuring her when they were talking of robbery and rape, and she was completely terrified?

She risked a glance at him, and her heart skipped a beat. Ibuka was white as a sheet. His hands were trembling on his katana and the weapon shook pathetically in front of him, a far cry from the perfect defensive stance he usually adopted. Drops of sweat trickled down his brow, and his eyes were aimed at the ground, as if he was already defeated. A urine stain spread across the front of his pants.

"Ibuka, what the hell are you doing?" screamed Atsuko before even having time to think. "We can beat them!"

"Your brother doesn't seem to agree," chuckled the leader while spinning his own katana. "In fact, I reckon he could faint at any moment. Wow, we live in such a great time, where women are braver than men—but with less brains. So leave us the cow and run away with your tail between your legs. I won't ask a third time."

"Maybe—maybe we should do what they say," murmured Ibuka, without daring to look his sister in the eyes. "It's just a cow, after all."

"It's just a—" she repeated, incredulous. "That's not the point! We won't let them get away with it! What would Father say?"

The leader started massaging himself in a suggestive manner in front of her.

"I've changed my mind. This spicy attitude is exciting. So, because you refuse to listen to reason, we'll make a woman out of you."

"Yeaah! My turn first!" exclaimed the brigand with the oversized breastplate.

"Why always you?" protested the one with the naginata.

"Because otherwise I break your arm."

Atsuko looked again at her brother. He was surely going to help her. Surely. He was her brother. The reincarnation of Miyamoto Musashi. The most promising swordsman in Aizu. But he stood there, completely still, tears streaming down his cheeks.

The teenage girl felt a wave of disgust wash over her—and suddenly a wave of fury. White hot fury. The world was so unfair. She did not want to find a husband in the house of the daimyo. She didn't want to be raped on a mountain trail. She didn't want to lose her katana. She didn't want to watch her brother whine and shuffle from one foot to the other.

Before letting herself think and determine whether it was a good idea, she bounded forwards, as if her years of training had taken control. Without even thinking, she delivered a tsuki to the throat of the brigand leader. He didn't see her coming and didn't block. His reflexes were nothing compared to Ibuka, and he didn't even see the blow that ended his life. Blood burst out, red and so much of it, so much. In a fraction of a second, Atsuko was soaked in it from head to toe. She had kept her mouth open in a battle cry, and she felt the metallic taste on her tongue.

"Hey!" cried the brigand with the breastplate, stupefied.

That was all he had time to say. She advanced, changed her defensive stance, raised her sword and slew him with a perfect *men-uchi*.* The man's breastplate was no use when his head stuck out like an overripe watermelon.

"Bitch!" growled the man with the lance.

He threw himself at her to pin her, but he too was much slower than Ibuka. She pivoted, deflected the lance with the flat of her sword and then thrust up an unorthodox sideways blow that penetrated her opponent's shoulder.

The man let out a wail and reflexively dropped his weapon to shield his face with his hands—which had no effect when the katana promptly sliced his head in two.

She turned to the others, but they were already backing away as though they'd seen a devil in their midst. She watched them flee, asking herself in confusion if she shouldn't chase after them to stop them doing the same to other travelers, when she suddenly remembered she was covered in blood. She staggered, tripped over something that she realized was the frowning head of her third victim looking at her from

* Blow from high to low.

the ground. She cried out and fell to her knees, trying to drop her katana, but the sweat and blood kept it glued to her palm. On all fours, she vomited once, twice, until all that was left was bile.

She stayed there for a while, her head lowered, her hair bun wrecked, and her long hair covered in blood and vomit. Finally, she got up.

Her brother still hadn't moved. He was in the exact same defeated position, and his haunted eyes were looking at the bodies as though he couldn't comprehend what had just happened.

"Ibuka," Atsuko said gently.

The young man jumped but did not respond. She put her hand on his shoulder, and felt the web of tension, muscles that were about to snap.

"Ibuka," she repeated in the same tone.

He turned towards her and seemed to finally come out of his trance. The katana dropped out of his hands and hit the ground with a soft thump.

"What happened?" he gasped. "What happened?"

His sister picked up the katana and handed it back to him. Then she picked up her own, swiped it through the air to clean the blood off it, and sheathed it in the same movement as she would in training.

"What happened, dear brother, is that you might be a genius swordsman, but you are also a damn coward," she responded icily. "Get the cow, we're going to be late home."

She gave one last glance at the three bodies in front of her, suppressed a shudder, and turned to make her way home. She didn't look behind to see if her brother was following.

4

In the fancy areas of Edo, wearing a katana was a mark of prestige. The samurai of the great families all fought to benefit from the services of the most famous blacksmiths, and they spent a fortune to obtain elaborate pommels or bronze scabbards adorned with precious stones to replace simple wood.

Matsuo's weapon was an impressive kind of ugly. He had kept the same katana for fifteen years to survey the many battlefields of the archipelago and the blade had been dulled by the armor of his enemies. Instead of changing the sword, he had it reforged. When the flat edge had been broken by getting hit from the side, he had collected the pieces and an artisan was brought in to fix the damage, even though there was still a crack on the left side of the pommel. All the courtiers could only hide their contempt of the result behind a polite smile.

On the other hand, any *other* courtier would have shuddered to see where Matsuo was headed.

He advanced at pace through the muddy streets of the north of the city with a smile on his lips. This was where the *burakumin*, the outcasts, lived and prowled the dark alleys. One man, even a samurai, presented an appealing target and rumors would quickly spread across the rooftops that the body of this new idiot would soon be found in the river.

But nobody bothered Matsuo and his hideous katana. They said he'd massacred any who'd tried to rob him—and *that he'd laughed during the fight*. But the burakumin didn't hold back out of fear. It was out of respect.

Matsuo didn't look down on them, or try to teach them their place, or hold his nose when he met them. He was a *ronin*, a samurai without a master, and he behaved as a man of the people. He didn't hesitate to sit down with them to share his rice wine—a badly fermented, far-too-strong drink, that he drank like water. And he proved he was just as critical as them about the little Emperor on his throne.

"I'm telling you, he's so bad in his political life that it's carrying over into the bed chamber. Since their marriage, she's still waiting to sheath his sword. And as usual, it's up to the Shogun to do the dirty work."

That was the type of joking that went down very well with the burakumin, especially when mixed with alcohol.

But tonight, Matsuo wasn't here to relax in a public house. He continued at pace, his face set. He turned onto the corner of Renderers' Street and knocked on the front of a hovel. One short knock, one long, two short.

He was answered by the sound of a bolt, and the door opened. A man dressed from head to toe in black, his face covered in cloth, stood aside to let him pass inside.

The first time Matsuo met Issa, he had joked about the shinobi's outfit. How could you pass unnoticed in such an outfit? Everyone would remember him in the street, and it would be impossible to disappear in a crowd.

He had since changed his mind. Matsuo didn't believe in the sorcery of the *shugenja** but he was forced to admit that Issa's clothing flirted with the supernatural. He could disappear in the shadow of a simple candle, scale buildings effortlessly or even free himself of chains by dislocating his limbs with the agility of a snake. And that was only what Matsuo had seen with his own eyes.

Luckily, the two were on the same side.

"The situation is catastrophic," stated Issa with no preamble.

"Catastrophic," confirmed Matsuo, dropping into the only chair in the house. "What is Tokugawa playing at?"

"He has no choice. The Emperor and the British are putting pressure on him."

* Men who possess a privileged contact with the spirit world and can command the kamis.

"So? This is Tokugawa we're talking about. He could just ignore them both."

Issa's eyes shone behind his half-mask, like a cat.

"He could, but to openly defy the Emperor would mean civil war and he has no desire for that."

"So, what? He's just going to let himself be walked all over with no pushback? Do you know what he's done? He's *abandoned his duties as Shogun!*"

Silence fell once more in the room as they both contemplated the implications of what they had learned the day before. They were both members of the Brotherhood of Assassins, which claimed to be the biggest network of information in the world. But even so, this piece of news had taken them completely by surprise.

Tokugawa had started by obeying the demands of the Emperor with no conditions. He had removed the governor of Nagasaki, provoking outrage amongst his troops. And finally, he had presented his resignation to the Emperor.

"This would never have happened under his father," growled Issa. "Sure, Nariaki had his flaws and despised Westerners, but he never would have abdicated like this. The worst is that nothing will change. The British won't let Tokugawa peacefully retire. Even if he leaves the Imperial court, his clan is far too powerful for them to ignore. Anyway, maybe that's exactly what the Shogun wants: to leave the vipers' nest and gather his forces to try a *coup d'état.*"

Matsuo frowned, doubtful.

"He'd never be brave enough. And his image is destroyed after all these humiliations. Some clans have decided to support the Emperor. If he ever tried to take over by force, civil war would be inevitable."

"At the very least, we could remove an element from the equation," suggested Issa in barely a whisper.

"What do you mean by that?"

The shinobi wrung his hands, and as if by magic, two *tantōs** appeared in his palms. They disappeared as quickly as they had appeared, but Matsuo had the time to see reflections of green on their tips. Poison.

"Tokugawa can't face the Emperor, the unhappy daimyos, and the machinations of the British Empire all at the same time. Even the Brotherhood wouldn't risk getting to the Emperor, and the daimyos alone wouldn't have enough impact to reverse the station. The English, on the other hand… their consul has proven to be very aggressive lately. If something were to happen to him, it would send an interesting message to all who oppose the Tokugawa clan."

Matsuo shook his head, still unconvinced.

"It would have the opposite effect. Everyone would think Tokugawa was behind it, and he'd find himself even more

* Small Japanese slightly curved dagger with a blade of less than twelve inches.

weakened. Look at what the British caused for two dead sailors. Imagine what they would do if their consul was murdered?"

"Quite right," chuckled Issa. "Tokugawa is no longer Shogun. He has left the Imperial palace. He's no longer responsible for the safety of guests, but the Emperor is. If the British want to find the guilty party, they would have to look to the guards of the court. Not to mention that we might get lucky with the new consul. If everyone who takes on the role is assassinated, they would undoubtedly be more cautious about meddling in our affairs."

"Or maybe they simply better protect themselves against assassination attempts."

Issa blew out the candle on the table, and without warning, disappeared into darkness. One moment he was there, and the next there was no one in the room.

"Leave it to me to sort the details. Infiltration is my domain. The Brotherhood has a special mission for you that's just as important."

Everyone at the castle knew Harry Parkes only needed four hours of sleep per night. The rest of the time he spent working or reading in his office.

In any case, that was the story that the consul wanted spread. The reality was that he felt permanently exhausted and would have loved to sleep for longer but suffered from severe insomnia. The English doctors could no longer treat him, and the plant remedies from the herbologists in Edo Castle no longer had any effect.

After tossing and turning in his bed, Parkes gave up the fight for the night. His mechanical watch showed two o'clock in the morning—the hour of the tiger. He got up, stretched, and shuffled towards the library. On the way, he greeted the guards patrolling the corridor. Trustworthy and dependable men, good Englishmen with unfailing discipline and well-groomed mustaches, and all armed with a rifle and a sword.

After the show of force by the Emperor and the departure of Tokugawa Yoshinobu, the situation was tense at the castle, and the patrols had been increased.

Parkes wasn't worried: who would dare to attack the consul of the most powerful Empire in the world? He yawned, rubbed his eyes to chase away the last traces of sleep, and sat heavily down at his desk. He still had three memos to write, and two reports sat awaiting his sign-off on the corner of the table. The pleasure of Her Good Majesty did not like to be kept waiting.

He shot an irritated look at the two British soldiers seated on a bench at the other end of the room. Even here, he had no right to any privacy. The only place he could be truly alone was the toilets—and that was only because there were no windows or openings to the outside.

"Well don't just sit there doing nothing," grumbled Parkes. "If you must keep me company, go and make me a tea. You should know how I like it after all this time."

The guards made no response and the consul frowned. Had they fallen asleep at their post? If that was the case, the punishment would be severe—even more so, sulked Parkes, because he himself had only managed five minutes of shut-eye. He raised his voice in irritation:

"*Pasambleu*, do I have to fire a shot to get a reaction? Get up this instant!"

Once more they did not respond, and a seed of worry was planted in the consul. He opened the bottom left drawer of his desk and pulled out a Colt Navy 1861 that he kept with him at all times. The weight of the metal in his hands calmed him instantly. The samurai could play with their katanas and think of themselves as incomparable warriors, but the real power came from guns. He would have liked to see their heroes, like this famous Miyamoto Musashi, try to go up against a good revolver.

He checked the gun was loaded and called out in a voice that was weaker than he would have liked:

"Anyone! Hello! Someone!"

He got a response almost immediately, but it wasn't the one he was expecting. Instead of his guards, William Lloyd was the one who answered, standing with his sword drawn and looking disheveled after running.

“Your Grace! Take cover!”

“What is the meaning...”

Parkes had no time to finish his sentence. Lloyd slammed into him with all his bodyweight and pushed him to the floor behind his desk at the same moment a projectile shot in his direction. Out of breath, and with the wind knocked out of him, the consul couldn’t tear his eyes away from the arrowhead that had embedded in the wood. A green liquid ran down the ebony carvings.

“You’re in danger!” clarified the Templar, rather obviously.

Upon impact, Parkes had dropped the Colt. He reached under the desk to retrieve it and almost lost two fingers as a blade came down just in front of his hand. He withdrew his arm with some words that weren’t entirely proper.

“Stay behind the desk!” ordered Lloyd, advancing forwards.

He cut the air with his sword before assuming a defensive position. Parkes couldn’t see his adversary and wondered if he was going crazy. Then, as his eyes adjusted to the darkness, he began to make out a wavy, almost smoky figure which seemed to travel using the shadows in the center of the room.

“William Lloyd,” hissed Issa. “I know you. I do not wish to fight you.”

“*No one* wants to fight me,” laughed the Templar. “But you have no choice. Tonight, I am your death.”

"I have a proposition for you," countered the other.

Lloyd hesitated for a split second and his sword dropped by a fraction of an inch. It was almost nothing, an almost imperceptible movement, but the shinobi seized the opportunity to clap his hands and throw two tantōs forwards. The blades flew: precise, deadly, and poisoned.

Lloyd spun his katana and his blade blocked the daggers one by one, deflecting them to the wall. He reestablished his defense, impassible.

"Your proposition wasn't very interesting."

"Look at your leg," replied the shinobi.

His face was hidden by the black fabric, but his eyes shone with a twisted joy. The tantōs were just a distraction. The real attack had come from the Assassin's mouth, a poisoned arrow launched by his tongue that had just broken through the fabric of Lloyd's trousers.

The poison was less concentrated than on regular weapons, and this dose would not be enough to kill, nor even paralyze a man of such size. But it would affect the nervous system, slow reflexes, and cloud the senses. Already, a tremor had started in the legendary swordsman's foot, destroying his balance.

"This poison will reduce your abilities times ten," explained Issa placidly, taking a step back to allow the liquid to take hold.

"Oh," rasped Lloyd.

Under the table, Parkes held his breath out of fear that the slightest noise would give him away. His hand was reaching inch by inch towards the revolver under the table. Everyone had forgotten about it, but if he could bring it into play against the intruder, no ninja powers could save him. The consul was a decent shot, and no one could survive a bullet to the head at this distance. No, he wouldn't risk a difficult target, he'd aim for the torso and that would be enough.

Just eight more inches… six… four…

Issa curled up like a cat, and he aimed the metal plaque on his left arm to reflect the candlelight into his opponent's eyes. Many were convinced that he had supernatural powers, but it was only training. A painful and pitiless training from childhood that allowed him to dislocate his limbs, hold his breath for several minutes—or to use any distraction to delve into the shadows.

Lloyd blinked his eyelids, momentarily blinded, disoriented, and slowed by the poison. Issa took advantage to strike. Another tantō appeared in his hands and he sprung forwards, aiming for the jugular.

The Englishman's sword moved with an improbable speed, and the knife dropped at the same time as the dismembered hand of Issa. The shinobi's eyes widened behind his mask, but the katana swung back in a pendulum motion, and cut through him as if the abdominal muscles he had built for years simply didn't exist.

"You're a great Assassin, but you're a terrible swordsman," choked Lloyd, his breathing hindered by the poison. "A tenth of my reflexes is enough against someone like you."

Holding his own entrails in his hand, Issa let out a nervous laugh.

Blood bubbled on his lips. Suddenly, his fabric mask was suffocating.

He would not succeed in killing the consul. He wouldn't end this night alive: it was regrettable, but every mission had its variables. There was still the secondary objective—despite his best efforts, Lloyd was affected by the poison. He would never be as vulnerable as he was currently, now that he thought he'd won.

Issa let himself fall backwards, rolled his eyes upward to make them look fully white. He crashed to the ground, lay awkwardly, and held his breath so as not to move a muscle.

His last attack had released a needle into his left hand, and he waited patiently for his opponent to come closer. A single scratch would double the poison dosage he'd received. This time, the paralysis would spread through his organs and cause certain death.

"Are you alright, Your Grace?" called Lloyd.

"Is he dead?" responded the consul.

"I would think so."

"Not good enough for me," insisted Parkes. "I've heard a lot about these shinobi. They have multiple lives and can be reborn from their own ashes. Don't get too close, and cut off his head."

It was so stupid that Issa almost laughed out loud. In the end, it was his reputation that would be his undoing. The ninjas had not hesitated in exaggerating their exploits to instill fear, and it had come back to bite him. In a last effort and despite his mortal wound, he got ready to strike. He opened his eyes, saw his target in front of him and raised his left hand to throw his arrow.

"What did I tell you?" said Parkes, coldly.

He stood behind his desk and had retrieved the gun. Issa had the time to register the enormous barrel of the revolver, then there was a deafening boom, and then he heard no more.

5

Normally, Atsuko loved autumn. The heat of summer dissipated into a welcome freshness, while fiery swathes of color invaded the countryside. Travelers returned to the capital, the peasants prepared for winter, and the streets of Aizu calmed. Her father was also more present in the family home and had more time to take care of the family.

But this autumn left a bitter taste in her mouth. Atsuko could not forget the cursed day on the road, and she could no longer look at her brother without shuddering in disgust.

The worst thing had been his reaction when they finally arrived at the edge of town after two hours of guiding the cow.

"Are—are you going to tell people what happened?" he had asked, his eyes on the ground.

"I don't know, what do you think?" she replied acidly.

He had fallen to his knees in front of her.

Him.

Ibuka.

On his knees.

In front of her.

"I beg you, don't tell anyone. I wouldn't survive such humiliation. No shogun would want anything to do with me. At best, I would have to leave town and become a ronin. Father would never live it down. He has put so much of his hopes on me."

"And he shouldn't have!" shrieked Atsuko. "Come on, get up, I'm the one you're making ashamed. But seriously, what the hell happened? How could you be afraid of them?"

"I don't know," he admitted in a trembling voice. "Genuinely, I don't know. I saw the blade of his katana and it all seemed so—real. He was right, you know, we spend all our time training in the dojo but it's no game. A single error and you're maimed for life. You have hopes and dreams—and the next second you fall to the ground in a sea of blood, and all your plans turn to smoke. None of the three brigands you killed were expecting it. They all died with an expression of such surprise on their faces. They must have had friends, family, and now nothing."

"And I have no regrets," insisted the young girl. "What are you trying to say, that we shouldn't have defended ourselves?"

"No, you did what had to be done. I have no excuse. But that's no reason to ruin my life and Father's."

Atsuko had been so furious that she could have stood on a soapbox in the middle of the Aizu market and shouted for all to hear about what happened. It was the mention of her father that stopped her—she had no desire to cause him pain and could too well imagine his injured expression and his dreams in ruin.

Plus, in a certain way, she pitied her brother. So, she had reassured herself that it was the best decision and that she would move on from the incident.

But two months later, the situation was worse.

She had had to watch him continue life as normal, admired by all for his talents with the sword while she wasn't even looked at, unless for the forms sprouting under her kimono. She had attended the evening at Matsudaira Katamori's residence, where Ibuka was the center of attention and gave a magnificent demonstration with a bokken to the cheers of the encircled samurai. She had wanted to scream at them that there was a mistake, that her brother was no hero, and that he hadn't lifted a finger to help her and pissed himself instead.

But no, she had smiled politely to all the courtiers who spoke to her, laughed at the right times, shook her hair in the right way, and proved herself to be the perfect daughter of a perfect father. The evening was a success according to everyone, and Ibuka had joined the ranks of the daimyo, a great honor at such an age. As for Atsuko, she had received two proposals of marriage that she promised to seriously think about, but she had managed to refuse to her father under the pretext that the suitors were not rich or well-established enough in the court.

But there was no time to waste, and she knew it all too well. Her brother was no longer there as a training partner, and to be honest, it was a relief to not have to see him every day. Sometimes she crossed him in the street marching with the other guards and he would hurry to avert his eyes and move the troop in a different direction.

And just when she thought her life could not get any more miserable, rumors of war arrived in Aizu.

Shiba Tanomo was almost always in a good mood, and his smile was almost as legendary as his huge shoulders and gigantic arms.

So when he came into the house with a pained expression and his brow furrowed, Atsuko knew it must be serious.

"Is everything alright?" she asked in a small voice.

"No," he replied. "Nothing is alright. Ibuka might—"

His voice broke and he stopped himself.

In a split second the teenage girl wondered if her brother had finally given himself away, if he'd proven his cowardice when someone approached him with a weapon. That would surely put her father in such a state. With surprise, she felt her heart break in two, and realized that she didn't want that for either of them.

"Ibuka might what?" she pressed.

Her father slumped on the carpet and took the time to calm his breathing. When he raised his head, he still wasn't smiling, but at least his eyes were no longer glassed over.

"The Emperor has betrayed all his obligations and attacked the Tokugawa clan, who had already agreed to retreat peacefully. Under the pretext of installing a strong government, Mutsuhito has decided to break the authority of the regional daimyos. Do you know what that means?"

Atsuko opened and closed her mouth a few times like a fish out of water. She had never been interested in politics and, anyway, what was decided in Edo usually only had a small impact on Aizu.

Here, the authority of the daimyo was absolute and was worth much more than decrees signed in hundreds of places.

But she didn't need to be well versed in military strategy to state the conclusion her father was expecting.

"War," she breathed. "War."

"Yes," confirmed her father. "And not just any war. A civil war, Japanese against Japanese, clan against clan. No matter who wins, the island will be in ruins. Who knows if we will ever get out of this madness."

"But we're far from the capital," tried Atsuko. "Maybe the fighting won't reach here? Maybe Matsudaira Katamori will stay neutral?"

Her father was already shaking his head.

"Katamori has honor, and he has sworn loyalty to the Tokugawa clan. He would never go back on his agreement and will march under his flag. Which means I will also march. Just like Ibuka."

He tried to contain his emotions, but his voice betrayed him.

"I had hoped you would make a good marriage before I left, but that won't be possible. What will you become if I do not return, or if your brother isn't here to protect you?"

Atsuko felt a wave of rage engulf her at these last words but sucked her teeth and held in her words like bad bile.

"When do you leave?"

"The day after tomorrow," was the murmured response. "We will join the armies from the Jozai and Nagaoka clans to meet with Tokugawa, then we'll make our way towards the capital."

The day after tomorrow. She suddenly felt sick. She took a deep breath and waited for her breathing to return to normal before speaking.

"Will you win?"

Most fathers would have looked their daughters in the eyes and told them that yes of course, it was for certain.

Some would have shown off their muscles, puffed out their chests and promised that the gods were with them. But Tanomo was not the type. He was a profoundly honest man, and he took a moment to give the truest answer he could.

"I don't know, my darling. The Emperor can count on the support of a few clans who oppose Tokugawa, like the Satsuma and the Shoshu clans. And of course, he's being pushed by the damn British. On paper, there are more of us, but the battle will be brutal—"

He stopped mid-sentence upon hearing the sound of steps in the entry. Atsuko looked up just in time to see Ibuka burst into the living room, as white as a sheet.

The effortless arrogance he normally showed in the streets had vanished and he was half shaking, like an old man with a drinking problem. His wild look landed on his sister, then onto his father, and he seemed to realize his haggard appearance. With a supreme effort of willpower, he readjusted, fixing the folds of his kimono and forcing his toothy smile.

"Father, have you heard the news?"

"You'd have to be deaf not to hear," grumbled his father. "I didn't think your first war would be so soon, but the *kamis** have decided. Let us hope they protect you during the battles as they have protected me for all these years."

* Divinity or spirit worshipped in the Shintoiste region.

Ibuka wiped his mouth. He was a good actor, and anybody who didn't know him so well would see no hint of fear on him, but Atsuko wasn't stupid. She could tell her brother was moments away from pissing himself again.

"If you hadn't presented me to the daimyo a few months ago, he never would have asked me to be his hatamoto," he observed in a detached voice. "I would still live here, under your roof, and I would have no obligation to swear loyalty to Katamori."

"That's true," agreed his father. "That evening came at the best possible time. You are the youngest of his guards, and the most talented. This will be the chance to cover you in glory at an age when other boys don't even know the meaning of the word. Musashi himself participated in the battle of Sekighara at age sixteen!"

"Yes, and his side lost, and he was left for dead," observed Ibuka before stopping himself.

"All the same, it's a question of honor," concluded his father. "We are defending not only our daimyo but our entire feudal system. If the Emperor takes the battle, then there will be no more caste, no more samurai. He has been trying to revoke our privileges for years. I've heard he even wants to ban the carrying of swords." He shook his head in disbelief at something so ridiculous. "We are lucky, my son: we will fight for something we hold dear. Not every samurai can say the same. I remember the senseless wars of my youth, over a tiny piece of worthless land or an insult between two prideful daimyos. Blood has already been spilled over futile pretexts, but this time we are writing history."

Ibuka bowed his head, not daring to respond. For the first time in months, Atsuko felt a hint of tenderness towards her brother. He was trapped, completely trapped, and she didn't envy his position. He would end up on the frontlines and wouldn't be able to control his nerves, so he'd either dishonor himself in front of the entire world or die at the hands of a more determined enemy.

"The daimyo has probably already told you, but we leave in two days," concluded Tanomo. "You are already grown, and I don't have much more advice to give you, but if I were you, I would make sure my equipment is up to good standards. I'd oil up my breastplate and bring a few provisions. Merchants always go along with marching armies, but their prices are shocking. Oh, yes, and try not to party too much with the other young samurai from the clan. Just before heading to war, your blood boils and men want to drink, visit pleasure houses and dance all night, but they certainly regret it when they wake up the next day."

"You are right as always, Father," replied Ibuka in a far-off voice. "I will try not to celebrate this war too much."

The recruiting sergeants had set up their tent right in the middle of town, where the jeweler Mikinosuke was normally found. He charged exorbitant prices but somehow managed to satisfy all the rich of the region. This time, his reputation meant no free passes and he had to hastily remove his stand to make room for the soldiers.

The samurai, elite warriors who were well protected, well trained, and well armed made up only a tiny portion of troops in the army. The majority of soldiers were peasants armed with whatever they could bring with them, the *ashigaru*.

As their only protection, they wore a helmet, and their only weapon was a lance, even though the use of guns was growing more widespread. On the front line and without any armor, they normally suffered terrible losses at each skirmish. However, that didn't stop boys of age signing up *en masse*. Some did it out of idealism, others to be sure of a hot meal, and others in search of glory. Most imagined that the life of a conqueror would be more exciting than breaking your back on a farm. Whatever the case, there was no shortage of volunteers.

"Surname, first name, age?" announced the sergeant for the hundredth time that day.

"Mori Taisuke," stated Atsuko, trying to put on her deepest possible voice. "I brought my *yari*."*

* Japanese lance around eight feet long, favored weapon of samurai.

She had spent hours perfecting her disguise. The beautiful hair her father loved so much had fallen to the floor with the cuts of the scissors, and she had worked meticulously on the boys' clothes she had so innocently worn these last years. A little cream had reddened her too-pale skin, but there was nothing she could do for her hairless chin. She had tightly wrapped bandages around her breasts so that the rise and fall of her breathing would not betray her.

Then she accentuated her posture to the point of caricature, her hands in her pockets, her back bent like a peasant used to toiling in the fields, her yari proudly brandished in front of her. For once, the bulging muscles in her arms worked in her favor. Her 'friends' Tomoe and Yasuhime thought her too masculine? Well, all the better!

She could have done away with half her subterfuge, as the recruiting sergeant didn't even look up at her face. Concentrating hard on writing, he traced the *kanji* with the air of someone who had only recently learned to write and was trying his hardest. Eventually he nodded his head in satisfaction, still without looking at her, and indicated for her to join the others.

"Very well, Taisuke. If you wish to say goodbye to your family, now would be the time. We leave tomorrow at dawn."

Atsuko hurried to follow the others to the base camp outside town, adopting the blasé air of someone who'd seen other towns before.

The first thing that stuck her was the enormous amount of people. She knew that Aizu was a huge city of tens of thousands of inhabitants. But even during festivals, not everyone joined together in the same place.

The camp consisted of almost a thousand soldiers who swarmed like insects around a cluster of gigantic tents. Several fires broke up the landscape, upon which pots of soup or stew bubbled.

The second thing that struck her was the noise. This entire little world was shouting joyously, laughing, joking, and getting to know each other in an unbearable cacophony. The soldiers knew they were all in the same boat and needed to trust each other on the battlefield, which made them want to talk, talk, talk without stopping—and loudly!

The third thing she noticed was the smell. She had always taken great care of her personal hygiene and benefited from a bath at the end of each training session. Nothing could have prepared her for the smell of a thousand bodies that had not enjoyed her privileged upbringing, and whose farm scents mingled with the smoke to produce the smell of burning toilets.

For a moment, she wondered what the hell she was doing here. If someone realized she was a girl, it would be a disaster, and dishonor for her and her family. Could she keep her secret? And did she really want to be on the precipice of the battlefield?

"Yes," she whispered to herself. "A thousand times, yes."

Better this than waiting patiently at the house for news of the battles, waiting to see a messenger and wondering if he would bring news of the death of her brother or father. And even better— if their army won, then she would only have wasted a few months of her life and could return to the same point, waiting to marry someone rich and well-connected within the court.

"Plus," she told herself, "I have to save Ibuka."

Atsuko had made the decision when her brother set off to join the daimyo, dragging his feet and not even looking back. All her anger towards him had faded, replaced by a tenderness and fear for his safety. He was just a lost child in a war that was too big for him, a child terrified by its possibilities. Okay, he was a coward. But so what? It didn't make him any less kind, less funny, less intelligent, or less skilled. But in the meantime, he needed his little sister— who would protect him if not Atsuko, should any other brigands decide to attack him on the way?

Whoever wanted to hurt her brother, even if it was the Emperor himself, she was ready to intervene.

6

Matsuo wrinkled his nose while looking at the contact in front of him. He thought himself a man of big ideas, and his time amongst the Assassins had prompted him to accept the more progressive ideas of the Brotherhood. He knew deep down that the value of people didn't come from their appearance, age, or gender: actions were the only thing that mattered. That was why he felt so at ease amongst the burakumin.

Nonetheless, he never would have believed that his link to the Aizu army would be a woman. No, not a woman. A *girl.* She was, what, twenty-two years old? Maybe even less.

"Have you finished looking me up and down?" she asked calmly.

She kneeled, perfectly at ease on the *tatami*, dressed in a *hakama*[*] and a cotton vest that tried not to accentuate

[*] Large folded trousers, traditionally worn by medieval Japanese nobles and, notably, samurai.

her gender. Everyone knew who she was: the only woman to be allowed to sign up, daughter of a high functionary of the province. She was a martial arts instructor and a young naginata prodigy.

But even so.

Twenty years old? Nineteen?

Matsuo realized he kept staring at her without responding, and he waved to cover his embarrassment.

"Forgive me, I thought you would be..."

"A man?"

"... different. But no matter."

"I think so, too."

Matsuo met the eyes of the young woman and what he saw reassured him. She had the eyes of a fighter, and after all, wasn't that all he had asked for? She would not pass unnoticed, but he had long since realized that the best was to disappear was in the brightest light. After all, Issa mastered all the camouflage techniques of the shinobi, but it hadn't saved him from a bullet to the head.

And Jules Brunet, the Brotherhood contact for Europe, was furious with recent developments.

"Do you realize the seriousness of the situation?" he'd raged. "The Templars have infiltrated the Imperial court and manipulated the Emperor like a puppet. They turned him against Tokugawa and against us. The British will never stop gaining influence. I've been pushing Tokugawa for years to give power back to the people, little by little, decree by decree, and now this war has ruined all our hopes. Now we have no choice. We must win this, and decisively. The Emperor must be removed and his armies dispersed to the four corners of the world. Only then can we let Japan be the master of its own destiny. With the fall of the Imperial dynasty, who knows? A republic could flourish here."

"Influenced by France, of course," commented Matsuo.

"Of course," confirmed Brunet distractedly. "But everything in its own time. The first step is to provide the support of the Brotherhood to Tokugawa. But discreetly. He must not know our objectives."

And that was how Matsuo found himself at the edge of each muddy region, having to deliver instructions to all his contacts. He would have much preferred to be on the battlefields, but he did not dispute orders, not when they came from Jules Brunet. The ronin wasn't afraid of anyone, but he couldn't help but shudder when the pale eyes of the Frenchman landed on him.

"Have you been on missions of protection before?" asked Matsuo sharply.

Takeko raised an eyebrow, the only sign of trouble or anger she was allowed to show.

"Bodyguard duty? You want me to play babysitter to some daimyo? That's below me."

"No mission is below you when it's for the Brotherhood," corrected Matsuo. "And if it's any consolation, my superior believes him to be the most strategic target of our contacts. That shows how much I'm trusting you."

"Bodyguard," Takeko repeated not holding back her disdain. "I hate that. My infiltration skills will be useless and instead of acting, you have to *re*act."

"In fact, it's more complicated than that. Am I to understand that the mission scares you?"

The young woman's eyes shot daggers. *She can hardly control her emotions. She is still young,* noted Matsuo with slight concern. Would she be up to the task?

"Do not seek to provoke me," snarled Takeko. "It's simply a waste of my talents, but I will accept your mission. Who must I protect?"

"A daimyo by the name of Saigo Kayano."

"Never heard of him."

"That doesn't surprise me. He's not famous or powerful or even very political. He only has a few troops and depends on the Satsuma clan, not Aizu."

"From what you're describing, I don't see why we should defend him. Why is he so special?"

Matsuo allowed himself a small smile.

"His katana."

"Excuse me?"

"His *katana*," repeated the ronin. "An inheritance passed

down in his family from first son to first son for almost five hundred years. An authentic Masamune."

Takeko sucked in through her teeth. She barely *mastered* the katana; even though she knew the basics of kenjutsu, she much preferred her naginata. Even so, she had heard about Masamune, the legendary swordsmith who lived six centuries prior. They said he was inspired by the kamis and that his creations possessed a life of their own. Takeko didn't know if it was all true, if the blades he forged could actually cut through rocks like paper, but even his name struck a romantic chord in her that she hadn't felt since her teenage years.

"How could a small, provincial daimyo get his hands on a Masamune? I thought there were fewer than ten left."

"You're too generous," he said. "Most of those are fakes. I know a clan chief in the Imperial court who insists he's got one, but I had the chance to examine it up close and it's nothing special. It's a beautiful piece for sure, a forgery of great talent—but it's not a true Masamune."

"And we're sure that the daimyo's is authentic?"

"Yes. But that's not the only reason we're interested in the katana. Wouldn't you figure, one of his ancestors found it amongst the ruins of Chiba Castle."

This time Takeko's discipline couldn't stop her from turning pale. She put her hands on her knees to stop them trembling and looked deep into Matsuo's eyes for confirmation.

"You mean to tell me...?"

"Yes," stated Matsuo softly. "The Brotherhood believes that this is the authentic katana of Miyamoto Musashi. And more importantly, the Templars believe it too. They will try to take it for their cause. Imagine the disaster—for the Emperor to stride into battle with Musashi's Masamune in hand. And not even to mention the incredible powers of such a weapon. The symbolism would be devastating. We cannot permit it."

"In that case, why don't we just take the sword for ourselves?" asked Takeko, her eyes wide.

"Because the symbolism would be even worse. Saigo Kayano fights for us, in the Tokugawa armies. What would the other daimyos think, if one of their own died and his legendary weapon mysteriously appeared in the hands of the Shogun? What example would that show?"

The young woman lowered her eyes in shame. She hadn't thought it through. But even so, Miyamoto Musashi's sword... She felt a shiver run from her toes up to her head in an almost mystic ecstasy.

"Well? Does your mission still seem so simple and useless?" laughed Matsuo.

"My naginata is yours," responded Takeko simply.

No Templar would touch this sacred weapon.

The most difficult part was the toilets.

For everything else, Atsuko had managed to adapt with impressive speed. She no longer smelt the stench—she hadn't washed for a week since the beginning of the march herself, in any case. The bandages compressing her chest continued to bring her suffering, but she had accepted the constant pain and didn't even pay attention to it anymore.

Thanks to her peak physical condition, she was easily able to keep up, and she paid close attention to keeping her voice deep and not speaking to people unless she had to.

But the toilets were still complicated—because most of the time there were none.

Normally, the ashigaru had to set up camp every night and include latrines, under very strict criteria. To avoid the spread of disease, they had to be at minimum of five *jo*[*] from the fires, which meant extending the ramparts to avoid bumping into enemies in the dark. All that to say that after a day's march, the soldiers had no desire to work more that was necessary and the latrines were forgotten about.

So the ashigaru peed standing against a tree, a rock, a log, or against a tent. They peed in front of everyone, without even interrupting their conversation and talking over their shoulder like it was completely normal. Sometimes two or three dropped their trousers at the same time, which would

[*] Five *jo* is the equivalent of around fifty feet.

provoke a contest to see who could aim the furthest or put out the fire. Distractions were few and far between on this march to war, and the soldiers had to change things up to avoid thinking about death.

So, they peed far, they laughed loudly, and told each other stories to joke and to frighten, awaiting the real terror.

And Atsuko found herself in the middle of these rowdy teenagers. Until now, she had avoided this type of display, but she had to scurry away in the night to urinate in secret in a corner of the camp, her heart in her mouth, always terrified she would be caught.

"Why did I do this?" she wondered miserably, waiting for the sentinels to pass before squatting behind them.

But she knew she was lying to herself. In reality, and despite these small details, she'd never felt so free, so happy. Nobody treated her any different than the others, and some had already complimented her skills with a yari.

From time to time, she spotted a glimpse of her brother or father in the adjacent camp. The samurai did not mingle with the lower classes and their tents were further away, more isolated, and much more luxurious. They certainly had toilets. Atsuko tried to imagine her father in a pissing contest and stifled a chuckle. There was no way in hell.

She rejoined her tent, as imperceptible as a ghost, and soon fell asleep, exhausted by the day's march.

The next day, while she was on the left of the column, she noticed her brother walking in the opposite direction, a weapon in hand, and with the air of someone important tasked with a mission. She took him in from head to toe; he looked wonderful in his breastplate, carrying his helmet under his arm. It was no surprise everyone took him for a legendary hero. She even began to wonder if she hadn't imagined it all, if the fight in the hills had really even happened.

Lost in her thoughts, her eyes lingered a second too long before she averted them, and Ibuka met her gaze, shocked by a soldier who dared stare at him that way.

Atsuko was well disguised, and her cut hair made her look completely different, but the two had lived together for sixteen years and everything that could fool a stranger had no effect on her brother. Ibuka stopped, as if stunned, his message forgotten in his hand.

Atsuko hastily tried to continue on her way, hoping he might think it was a hallucination, but of course, it was too much to hope. She felt a hand on her shoulder that guided her out of the column.

"You there," called Ibuka in the commanding voice he'd normally use for all subordinates. "You seem strong. You will help me carry these crates to the intendant.'

"But..." began Atsuko before stopping herself.

No ashigaru could ignore a direct order from a samurai and even less so under the watch of the sergeants. She lowered her head as a sign of submission to follow her brother.

He marched at speed for a good minute then hid from the column behind a cart of crates which would make for his alibi. Finally, he turned towards his sister with a furious expression. There was no trace of his usual cheesy smile.

"By all the kamis, what on Earth are you doing here? And in those clothes? And your hair? And... and... have you gone completely insane?"

Atsuko folded her arms; now that no one was watching, she could let herself answer him.

"I wasn't going to stay in Aizu while you all went off to fight," she explained calmly. "No way I'd sit going out of my mind waiting for news, all while rejecting marriage proposals from men who weren't brave enough to fight."

"But that's no reason!" gasped Ibuka, sounding like a strangled cat. "You know what I think about you, you're more skilled than many men, but the law is the law. Girls aren't allowed to join the army, and if anyone discovers your secret, you'll be in grave danger."

"I saw a woman in the army," protested his sister. "Her name is Takeko and she's amazing. They say she masters the naginata better than anyone."

"She's the exception to the rule. Even her presence makes things complicated for us. We can't..."

"... what, piss in front of her?" she finished, with malice. "Oh, I'm sure."

"That's not the point," said her brother. "Father must not know you're here; it would kill him. I'll see what I can do to have you sent back to Aizu discreetly."

Until now, Atsuko had contained herself, but this time she headed straight for him, wagging her finger until she squared up to him.

"You'll send me nowhere! It so happens that I like this life, that I feel free for the first time in months—ever since Father talked about that night with the daimyo and my future marriage, in fact. And that's not all. I signed up for you."

"For me?" Ibuka repeated incredulously.

"How will you do on the battlefield? I don't want to worry you, but the enemies will have real katanas with real blades that will cause real injuries. If you act like you did in the hills, you'll be killed in the first few seconds. And oddly enough, in spite of your cowardice, I still love you, big brother."

"Don't you talk to me like that!" he yelled, shaking with rage. "I've told you a thousand times, what happened was an accident. Next time I'll be different. I spend an hour every night fighting with the other samurai and I've never lost."

"Yeah, with a bokken," she added. "Look, I hope you're right. Maybe you will find your courage at the right time, and you'll become the hero everyone expects. But while we wait to be sure, I plan to watch over you."

"And how will you do that as an ashigaru? We won't be in the same place."

"That's where you're wrong. I've worked hard and done many favors to be placed on the west wing, where you'll be too. You can count on me, big brother."

Issa massaged the bridge of his nose as though he felt a migraine coming on.

"Out of the question. I'll have you sent home, and that's that. I already have a hard enough time looking at myself in the mirror. I could never live with myself if you were killed on the battlefield. It's not your place."

He turned to indicate the conversation was over, but he didn't see the fire in his sisters' eyes as she shot a venomous look.

"If you try to have me sent away, I will tell everyone that I am your sister, and that I came to protect you from the scary enemies because you have no bravery in a fight. Oh, of course, no one will believe me. After all, you're a hero, a genius with a katana. They'd laugh me out of town. But that's how a seed of doubt gets planted. Some will ask questions and start to watch you more closely. Not to mention that they'd wonder if a samurai who can't control his own sister would be able to command soldiers on the battlefield."

"You wouldn't dare," gasped Ibuka, affronted.

"I would never do that to my brother," explained Atsuko in an even tone. "But if you send me home after I begged you not to, you would no longer be my brother, just a coward who didn't defend me in the hills as I was about to be raped.

So? What will you choose? Can I rejoin my troop, or are you sure you want to tell on me?"

Ibuka bit his lip and looked at her. He hesitated, though he knew he'd already lost. His sister was right: such accusations would be disastrous and would show him in the wrong, even if nobody believed it. He could not allow such a blow to his promising career.

And with some surprise, he realized that it would be a great comfort to have Atsuko with him on the battlefield.

Takeko waited for the samurai and the ashigaru to separate and rejoin their respective regiments, and then came out of her hiding place behind the food crates a little ways away from their position. She had not dared to get closer for fear of being spotted, and she hadn't heard their content of their conversation, but the fact that the two soldiers were discussing something for fifteen minutes was in itself very interesting.

She knew the first one well, a supposed legend of the samurai, Matsudaira Katamori's youngest bodyguard. She'd heard a few things around the fire—some compared him to no less than Miyamoto Musashi!

As for the other one, Takeko had never crossed paths with him—but that wasn't surprising as she didn't mix with peasants. But when she looked him up and down, she had the strangest feeling, like she was missing some key detail, something crucial but well-hidden.

What could these two possibly have in common? They had no reason at all to talk, which meant that they must be plotting something.

Could they be Templar agents?

Takeko slung the sheath of her naginata over her shoulder like a butcher carrying a pig, and quickly returned to the camp.

It was time to run surveillance on this mysterious ashigaru.

7

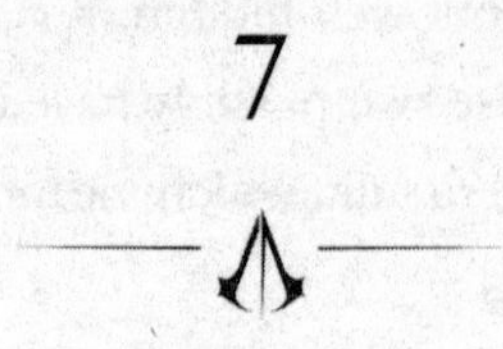

The nine samurai were veterans who had gained their reputations on numerous battlefields. They had all killed for the Templars' cause, even though they mocked the ideology of their employers. What mattered to them was that they were paid, and paid well. They had renounced their honor years prior: Saizu was betrayed by his daimyo, Yoshisada woke up under a pile of bodies with no memories. Masajiro, with his sweet smile, had been found guilty of seducing a courtier's wife. Nobusuke had razed an entire village in a fit of anger.

They were all disillusioned and jaded ronin who had looked death in the face, and now nothing else could ever impress them. They were bloodhounds in a world of sheep.

But even so, they kept their distance from their current commander. Because even dogs avoid the wolves.

"Is that understood?" repeated William Lloyd. "The mission should be uncomplicated. Saigo Kayano is only a minor daimyo, and he has no special protection. He's not expecting an attack."

"He is camping in the middle of his army," observed Yoshisada. "We aren't shinobi, we're warriors. We can't disappear into the shadows after our kill. We'll have to fight our way out."

"How many men does Kayano have?" asked Saizu, studying the map provided by Lloyd.

"About forty poorly armed soldiers, surrounded by five samurai."

"Nine against forty-five? Even for us that's a complicated fight."

The Templar let out a snort of derision.

"Don't make me laugh, Saizu. Most of their fighters are peasants with no armor. You could decapitate three before they even realized what was happening. You'll have the element of surprise—do you really think they'll continue fighting as you charge at them like wild animals once their master is dead and his bodyguards are lying with their guts hanging out?"

"Well, when you put it like that..." murmured Nobusuke while caressing the hilt of his katana.

"In any case, I don't pay you such healthy sums for you to stand there with your arms folded. If you don't want to work for me, I'll find other ronin."

"Whoa, let's not jump to hasty conclusions," protested

Masajiro. "I'm in. We attack the camp, we wreak havoc, kill the daimyo and take his sword. Why his sword, by the way?"

Lloyd hadn't thought it prudent to tell these idiots about the real origins of the sword. The Templars' money bought their loyalty, but he didn't want to risk talking about Musashi. Some would sell their mother and father to get their hands on such an artefact.

"We think it might be a Masamune," he started. "We will need to verify it, of course, but if it really is one of the blades of the master swordsmith, it would be a great psychological victory for the Emperor to recover it."

Nobusuke's eyes lit up, and Saizu unconsciously licked his lips. Even without talking about Musashi, the very mention of a Masamune had transformed the samurai. They stood straighter, sizing each other up as though they were now competing, their greed shining in their eyes.

Of course, Lloyd had anticipated their reactions. He had relative confidence in the men he'd gathered. It was their skill that came at a price, not their loyalty.

"I will be coming with you," he continued with a cold smile. "You were asking if you'd be able to beat your enemies, so my presence should reassure you."

Saizu frowned at the realization he wouldn't get his hands on the Masamune, but he had always been a pragmatic man.

"With you as our leader, the fight is already won. I pity the daimyo's soldiers."

For over two hours Takeko observed the soldier who'd talked with Ibuka, and she had not yet noticed anything strange. But her instinct continued to whisper that she was on the verge of a significant discovery.

She had discreetly asked around about him with a sergeant and learned some extra information. The ashigaru had joined the army in Aizu around two weeks ago. His name was Mori Taisuke. Takeko had never heard of the Mori family, but that was no surprise, as she never mixed amongst the peasants who swarmed around the city.

"An excellent recruit," confirmed the sergeant confidently, flattered that the only woman in the camp was speaking to him. "He's not a very good shot, but he's particularly skilled with a yari. He's either a genius or he trained a lot as a kid. Anyway, I've asked him a couple of times to assist me in exercises. He's not very strong, but he makes up for it with impressive flexibility and speed."

"And how does he get on with others?"

The sergeant scratched his head, perplexed.

"What do you mean?"

"Well, does he have many friends, does he mix a lot with the others, does he play cards at night, or does he bet a lot?"

"No, he's quite discreet. Not secretive, you understand, just… I don't know, shy. Solitary. You're really interested in this Taisuke, huh? Is there a problem? Should I watch him?"

Takeko bit her lip. She had no desire for this brute to spread her questioning to everyone. It would surely come back to the wrong ears, and if the soldier was indeed a spy, he'd disappear into the night as soon as he felt like he was about to be discovered.

There was only one way out, and as much as she hated it, Takeko was professional enough to use all weapons at her disposal.

"Oh, don't make me say why this boy interests me." She blushed. "He's good-looking and I find him charming. To be perfectly honest, all these questions were only me building up to the most important one: do you know if he has a fiancée in Aizu?"

The sergeant completely relaxed. He'd been afraid of getting caught up in some dodgy business, but suddenly he was in familiar territory. He winked with complicity.

"I don't normally ask my men that type of question, but I can find out. Discreetly, of course. I didn't know the famous Takeko could—"

"Could what?" asked the young woman icily.

"Could—could—" stuttered the man without knowing how to finish his sentence in the most innocent way. "Um, I have to go. I promise I'll have the answer before this evening."

He fled as though he had the devil at his back, while Takeko turned her attention to Taisuke.

The boy was training with the yari against an opponent who was over a head taller than him, and as the sergeant said, he held his own very well. Most peasants knew how to wield a yari but only to chase away wolves and predators that invaded their fields. Taisuke had clearly spent time in a dojo, however.

"You're careless, my boy," whispered Takeko. "A better spy would have hidden his talents to avoid being found out."

She slunk back into her shadow for more surveillance, not entirely sure what she was hoping to find out. She heard the faraway sound of the sergeant talking with the other officers and their laughter carried all the way over to her position. The sergeant was taking great pleasure in telling everyone that the terrible Takeko had a heart, after all.

Well, if it amused them, so what? Anything that could humanize her and make her more likeable would give her an advantage in future missions. But all the same, it was frustrating to be labelled so easily.

Two hours later, Takeko still hadn't noticed anything out of the ordinary. After training, Taisuke went directly back to his tent, only to reappear a little while later to prepare his equipment for the next day's march. A model soldier.

Defeated, the young woman saw the sun dropping behind the hills. She had wasted an entire day of rest chasing smoke. It was time to head back to the samurai camp and get a good meal. She couldn't allow herself to waste time like this.

She was just about to leave when Taisuke looked around far too nonchalantly, then got up with an over-exaggerated movement. He was attempting to move unnoticed but was trying so hard that it had the opposite effect. Fascinated, Takeko sunk back into the shadows and continued her surveillance.

The ashigaru disappeared behind a tent and headed towards the forest. Feeling that she was finally onto something, the young woman endeavored to follow him. When she wanted, she could be as silent as a panther, a shadow among shadows. Her armor didn't clink, and she held her naginata out so that the sheath didn't scrape the ground.

As he reached the edge of the woods, Taisuke turned sharply, and the young woman froze, pressed up against the side of a tent. She waited three heartbeats before continuing her pursuit.

She had barely entered the forest before she was enveloped by the dark of the night. The lights from the camp were no longer visible from here and the moonlight couldn't penetrate the thick foliage. She could only see a few yards in front of her and clutched her naginata tightly. What if it was a trap? What if…?

"Oh," she breathed upon reaching the clearing.

Taisuke was crouched behind a bush, and it took a few seconds for Takeko to realize what she was seeing. Knocked off balance, she tripped over a dead branch. The soldier jumped up and pulled up his pants, but it was too late: her secret had been revealed.

And what a secret!

"Incredible," started Takeko. "You..."

She couldn't finish her sentence. Taisuke's yari came towards her face, and she ducked at the last second, more out of reflex than will. The two blades clashed violently, and Takeko automatically replied with a thrust to the face. Taisuke dodged the tip that could have punctured her carotid by a finger's width. She dropped to the ground and kicked her legs to knock down her opponent, a clumsy movement that Takeko had no trouble dodging.

"Wait, I don't want to hurt you!" protested the latter.

Waste of time. The ashigaru attacked once more with the desperation of a wounded animal; she wasn't bad—she was fast, precise, efficient, and no doubt would have the upper hand over many opponents. But Takeko was practically born holding a naginata and had spent years mastering her art. She blocked all attacks from the opponent before getting into the defensive stance and kneeing her in the groin.

Any man would have doubled over, incapable of moving for several minutes with their testicles in agony. But Taisuke was no man. And the blow only sent her to the ground in pain for just enough seconds for Takeko to disarm her and put her naginata to her throat.

"I don't mean you any harm," Takeko repeated. "Calm yourself."

Slowly, the young woman previously named Taisuke slowed her breathing and calmed down. Takeko raised her unarmed hands as a sign of peace and stared at her captive.

"What made you want to pass for a man? No, let's start at the beginning. What's your real name?"

Her captive hesitated for a moment, trying to find a credible lie, and then her shoulders sagged.

"Atsuko," she admitted.

"Very pretty," said Takeko. "What made you pass for a man?"

"Because women aren't allowed in the army," she replied sulkily. "Except you. And I'm not you."

Takeko nodded her head slowly. Now that the initial surprise was over, she liked this girl in front of her. She hadn't hesitated for a moment to attack Takeko to preserve her secret, which showed a useful temperament.

And especially because she was saying what Takeko believed deep down: why stop women from becoming soldiers if they wanted to?

But whatever she felt for Atsuko, that didn't mean she had any sympathy for a spy.

"My next question will be decisive, so think hard before you reply," whispered Takeko, pushing a little pressure on her naginata. "What is the nature of your relationship with Shiba Ibuka?"

Again, that hesitation, as though the captive was searching for a lie, and once again the inescapable truth was written all over her face.

"My full name is Shiba Atsuko. Ibuka is my brother."

Takeko had expected a few things—she had even imagined a tragic love story, a desperate fiancée who'd signed up to be close to her beloved—but she had never dreamed such an answer, though she had no doubt that it was true.

"Your brother? Really?"

"Yes," sulked the teenager, averting her eyes. "We underwent the same training in the same dojo with the same instructors. I'm the first to admit he's more skilled with a katana, but I can hold my ground better than most boys my age. And despite that, he was sent to the front with the honor of being a daimyo's bodyguard while I was supposed to wait at home for a good marriage. I—I couldn't accept the life that was mapped out for me, so I signed up."

Takeko sensed that she wasn't telling the whole story, but it was close enough to convince her. And that explained the long conversation with Ibuka. The young woman couldn't stop smiling. She would never have dreamed of stumbling on someone so like her in the woods.

"You are very skilled, Atsuko," she said. "You know how to wield a katana and a yari. How well do you do with a tantő?"

"It's not my weapon of choice, but I do alright," replied the captive in surprise.

"We can already see that you have mastered the art of disguise, and you know how to pass for somebody you're not. You're skilled at lying and you know how to divert others' attention away from you, otherwise you'd already have been found out."

"You saw through it," replied Atsuko bitterly.

"Only because you were careless and talked to your brother. Without that, I never would have suspected you. Anyway, you're an intelligent girl and your many talents could be of use. What would you say about working for me?"

8

In a society that judged largely on appearances, Saigo Kayano was a historical anomaly. His clan had once held a certain power, but his ancestors had let the warlords take over their lands, and though the fields left to reign over were still prosperous, the clan was a modest one, with no memories of former glory. And Kayano certainly wouldn't be the one to change that.

The daimyo ate enough for four people, drank enough for four and slept for four. At seven feet tall, he could have been a giant, but the fat had long overtaken his bones. Barely thirty years old, he resembled an enormous panda whose protruding stomach hung out of his kimono and prevented him from buckling the fastenings of his armor for official ceremonies.

His clothes were permanently stained with *saké* or sauce, and his rare appearances in Edo had not left a good impression with the Imperial courtiers, which had diminished his status even further. Bound by honor, most of his hatamoto had stayed with him, but some had finally left to find a master more worthy of their sword in the name of the same honor.

Kayano had withered arms, a wilted kimono, and wilted honor—the only thing that shone brightly in his presence was the katana he wore permanently at his side. In his youth he had been a passable swordsman, but today he could barely unsheathe his weapon without dropping it. Nevertheless, he was extremely proud of it; it was a relic of the past that made him feel like he was still important in this world he no longer understood.

News of the war had taken him completely by surprise, and he was even more surprised to find that he had no good reason to ignore his Shogun's orders. He'd had to abandon the comfort of his lodgings for the dust of the road and trade his comfortable bed for a cart which, although it was piled high with cushions, kept bumping him about. He had to abandon feasts for scarce rations, and endure everything without his concubines, his musicians, his personal chef, and his alcohol reserves.

A month into the campaign, Kayano had lost fourteen pounds and a great deal of his patience.

"When we finish this," he droned, while contemplating a sad piece of meat sliding around his plate, "we'll have a good battle, we'll crush the Imperial forces and we can go home.

Hmm, or maybe we should have a banquet in Edo to celebrate our victory. That would be worth it. Yes, come to think of it, that's an excellent idea. But our generals are too timid. Instead of marching to battle, they're wasting our forces on pointless skirmishes. If it was up to me, I'd advance directly to the capital. There are more of us—they'd tremble in their boots."

"They've reinforced the ramparts and have many cannons, not to mention the English influence," replied one of his bodyguards respectfully. "A siege would be long and bloody."

"So? We have to do what must be done. Don't you think this campaign has already been *long and bloody*? Not like this piece of meat, which is overcooked. If it was up to me, the cook would be whipped in public."

Kayano often repeated the phrase "*if it was up to me.*" Alas, nothing was up to him, and he was well aware of it. He turned in fury as one of his soldiers opened the flaps to his tent, standing in mud-covered boots. The daimyo hadn't spent all day avoiding the weather for it to be brought near his bed.

"What now?" he grumbled. "Have you all decided to disobey me today?"

"A thousand apologies, Master, but a woman is here to see you."

"A woman?" repeated Kayano, suddenly interested.

There were only men surrounding him, he was well placed to know. Normally an army on campaign attracted its fair share of prostitutes, female herbalists and merchants, but the Aizu forces had imposed a forced march and prevented any from entering into the camps—to the great disappointment of the daimyo. The only woman he'd heard about here was...

"Lady Takeko," he hurried to address her while pathetically trying to get up from his reclined position.

Technically, she should have been the one to bow to him, but he was just so happy to see someone of the fairer sex after all his days of distress. He smoothed his beard with the back of his hand and readjusted his kimono. Even with his recent weight loss, he still couldn't suck in his stomach enough to close the final buttons.

"Master Kayano, thank you for agreeing to see me so quickly," stated Takeko, taking her turn to bow.

She was a true professional and she managed not to crack a smile as she took in the person she was bound to protect. She had researched him, of course, but it was one thing to read the reports and a very different one to meet the one carrying the legendary Masamune in person.

"I wasn't aware that we had a meeting scheduled, but I am delighted," started Kayano with his best attempt at a seductive voice.

He had a beautiful voice—that was something no one could take from him—but his lewd smile ruined the effect. He absent-mindedly stroked the sheath of his katana, then shifted from one foot to the other, not used to being stood for so long.

"Oh? Daimyo Katamori did not tell you?" asked the young woman in surprise. "Our spies have learned of a plot against your life, and I have been tasked with your permanent protection. That's all we know for now."

"You've been assigned to me?" Kayano half-shouted in joy, before finishing his thought. "Wait, what do you mean, a plot against my life? What does that mean?"

Takeko shrugged her shoulders.

"I am simply happy to obey, Master. I don't have all the details. But it seems as though that sword you carry has attracted some unwanted attention."

"The Masamune?" gasped Kayano, placing his hand on the bronze hilt encrusted with precious stones he'd commissioned specially. "I'm not surprised. Twice already in the last few years, men have broken into my compound and my forces removed them. All that over a sword!" He frowned. "Wait, we're in the middle of a military camp. Who would dare to attack me here? Is this a joke? More than a thousand soldiers are gathered around me!"

"Once more, Master, I just obey my orders. We don't know what our enemies are capable of. Maybe they've placed traitors in the camp, or maybe they have shinobi powers. All I know is that we will stop this attempt, no matter what it takes."

Kayano let himself fall back onto his bed. The worry that had crept up on him while the young woman was speaking ebbed away little by little. No matter the rumors, he felt safe here. That was the only advantage of being on the road. And he was going to benefit from the protection of the only woman in the whole camp. Okay, maybe she wasn't wholly to his taste, but in times of drought, he wouldn't turn his nose up.

"Allow me to introduce the men in charge of your safety alongside myself," continued Takeko impassably.

"Men? I thought you would be alone," protested the daimyo, his dreams in tatters.

"Believe me, we take this threat very seriously. Four samurai will accompany me and will follow your movements day and night. And allow me to present my lieutenant, Mori Taisuke, one of our finest fighters."

On Takeko's signal, Atsuko also entered the tent. She still couldn't believe what was happening. Just a few days ago, she was still playing incognito in the army and was satisfied with watching over her brother and father from afar.

But since she met Takeko, her life had changed completely. The young woman had given her lessons on disguise to accentuate her masculinity, had trained her with a naginata to consider her potential, and even fought her with a bokken—the teenager had come out of the duel with the upper hand, and instead of getting angry, Takeko had roared with laughter before congratulating her.

The next fight, with Takeko and her naginata against Atsuko with a bokken, had turned out much more balanced and the two young women had circled each other for a long time looking for an opening. Both of their defensive stances were perfect and though the naginata had a longer reach, the bokken was more precise. Takeko had eventually won the fight, but she saw her new recruit in an increasingly respectful light.

"I'd thought about training you for longer, but I want to see what you can do in the field," Takeko had finished, while wiping the sweat from her brow.

"They've asked me to protect a daimyo in case of an attack. The simple fact of me being there should dissuade the enemy, and I don't think we'll have to fight, but it will show me if you're capable of permanently maintaining your disguise when surrounded by bodyguards that are more intelligent than the soldiers in your camp. If one of them realizes you're a woman, I'll protect you from repercussions by saying it was my idea—but I will consider your mission a failure, and I'll remember it. Is that clear?"

"Very clear," replied Atsuko, nodding without thinking. "But I don't understand why I have to do all of this. These lessons in disguise and combat, what are they for? Who do you work for?"

The young woman simply smiled, but the humor didn't quite reach her eyes.

"For the moment, you don't need to know. All that matters is that I know your secret, and I could reveal it if you don't do what I say." Then she softened a little and added, "But I promise you won't regret it. I can see an incredible potential in you, and I know you will do great things. Isn't that what you've always wanted?"

The teenager was forced to admit it—she obeyed Takeko only partly due to her threats. The other part was out of respect, admiration and envy for this woman who was so free in a man's world.

"Hm, he doesn't seem very strong," observed Kayano, bringing Atsuko sharply back into the present. "Is he really your lieutenant?"

"As I told you, four other samurai will be present," replied Takeko patiently. "But I think you will be pleasantly surprised by Taisuke's talents. He will remain by your side at all times and will give his life to save yours."

"That's all I ask from any of my bodyguards," murmured the daimyo. "But this doesn't matter. Just how long until this supposed attack takes place? Don't tell me you'll be watching me for months."

"Rest assured, we will soon join the Nagaoka and Jozai armies, along with our French allies. Once we have combined, you will be untouchable. But in the meantime, we prefer to take all the necessary precautions."

Atsuko's disguise was particularly effective, especially thanks to Takeko's techniques, and no one doubted for a second that she might be a woman.

Luckily too, because Kayano's presence was insufferable as it was. If he had known her gender, things would have grown complicated very quickly.

But there was one person her disguise could not fool, and she knew she would soon have to face him. With a heavy heart, she saw his shadow making a path through this section of the camp. He moved like a cat, and the katana at his side acted as a simple extension of his body. He oozed an air of confidence that gave him the appearance of natural authority; when she saw him, Atsuko once again wondered whether she'd imagined what happened in the hills.

"What the hell are you doing here?" whispered Ibuka, grabbing her by the arm. "I was out of my mind worrying when I didn't see you in the camp anymore! I thought you'd been found out and they'd thought you a spy or tortured you or worse!"

"Sorry, they reassigned me to the protection of a daimyo and it was all done in the night. It seems he's received death threats and the army takes it very seriously."

Her brother looked at her in suspicion.

"And they asked you to protect him? You? I could understand them asking esteemed swordswoman Shiba

Atsuko, but why would they be interested in clumsy new recruit Mori Taisuke?"

A few days ago, Atsuko would have crumbled under her brothers' gaze in a few seconds; she had never been able to hide anything from him. But she had changed a lot recently and she shrugged her shoulders with a hint of indifference.

"I'm not as clumsy as you think. The sergeant said I was the best in the unit with a yari. Plus, it's not my job to ask questions. Nakano Takeko herself asked me to join the daimyo's bodyguards. What was I supposed to do? Refuse?"

"No, of course not," admitted her brother begrudgingly. "But you should have let me know all the same. I was out of my mind with worry. I almost told Father!"

Atsuko's heart skipped a beat, but no, he said *almost.*

"I'm sorry, you're right, I should have gotten a message to you. But I'm permanently at the daimyo's side and it's not easy to slip away, and even harder to keep my secret."

"I've heard about him." Her brother frowned. "They say he's just a pig who exists only to eat and seduce women. He hasn't tried anything with you, has he?"

"No, don't worry. Remember, to him, I'm a man."

"All the same..."

Ibuka hesitated for a moment and suddenly spotted Takeko, who had been watching them from afar, not intending to get involved. Ibuka cleared his expression and moved towards her. He bowed low and saluted her with the same politeness, despite their difference in rank.

"Lady Takeko, it's always a pleasure to cross your path in the camp. I have a request, if it is not too presumptuous."

"Shiba Ibuka, your presence is an honor for us. I have heard all about your exploits and I'm sure you will be one of the heroes of this war. What can I do for you?"

"I heard that daimyo Kayano has received death threats and that you are in charge of his protection, is that correct?"

Takeko looked him up and down and there was no longer any trace of softness in her eyes.

"That's correct. You are remarkably well informed."

"In this case, with the agreement of my master, I would like to join Kayano's bodyguard. It would be a terrible catastrophe if the enemies succeeded in breaching the heart of our state and I have come to humbly offer my katana to your services."

Atsuko cried out, much higher in pitch that Taisuke should have been able to, and stepped back, aghast. What was her brother playing at? Takeko barely blinked. The request must have taken her by surprise, but she recovered herself with impressive speed.

"Who am I to refuse such a weapon? If your daimyo allows it, then of course you have my blessing. And Kayano will be delighted to have a protector as famous as you."

Ibuka bowed once more and took his leave. At the risk of compromising her disguise, his teenage sister ran after him.

"What are you doing?" she protested. "Why are you joining my mission like this? Don't you think I'm capable?"

"Of course I do," replied her brother. "I'm the first one to know that you don't back down from anything. A curse on the enemies to try to attack Kayano. But—I don't know, I think it would be good for us to be in the same place. If things were to go bad, I'd be at your side to protect you."

"Oh really?" asked Atsuko, dubious.

"Plus," he continued in an even tone, "I'm starting to get bored of the endless training sessions, and I bet this mission will be perfect. Daimyo Kayano is known for his well-stocked wagons, and I could have a nice break here with you."

"And what if enemies do attack?"

The young man burst out laughing and pointed to all the sentinels along the different entry points.

"I don't know who made up this story of threats, but do you really think someone will try and break in to such a fortified camp? It's a big joke, but it gets me the most peaceful post I could have hoped for during this war. While the other samurai are trudging through the mud and rain in fear of the enemy, I'll be warm and dry travelling in a wagon. I couldn't have dreamed of a better situation."

Of course, Ibuka was wrong.

Because the nine samurai were only three leagues away.

9

In the morning, the warriors were fresh, ready to face the long day of marching that awaited them. Even though some were only half awake, their tiredness would vanish under attack. It wasn't the best moment for an ambush.

During the day, the soldiers advanced in their long column which stretched across the horizon, while the sergeants on horseback rode back and forth to keep ranks in line and scouts surveilled every direction. It wasn't the best moment for an ambush.

At night, camp was set up and the palisades erected. There were fewer sentinels, but those that remained were more attentive, and you would have to possess the powers of a shinobi rather than the brute force of a samurai to get past them. The slightest error could provoke a terrible ruckus and wake all the soldiers, making for a desperate fight—not to mention the difficulty of escaping in total darkness. It wasn't the best moment for an ambush.

In the evening, the soldiers gathered to build the fences as ordered by their sergeants. They were tired, in a bad mood, and pushed by sergeants who were just as exhausted as them. The long march had worn down their legs, they hadn't eaten yet, and all they could think about was resting in front of the fire. Discipline was lax, tempers flared and there were many arguments. Soldiers split into smaller groups to find wood, or to dig trenches for the infamous latrines. Darkness also began to descend on the camp fortifications, making infiltration without giving away their movements much easier.

This was the perfect moment for an ambush.

"We get in, we strike, get the katana and get out. No overzealousness, no misplaced heroism, no sunset duels, no time wasted. Kill anyone who gets in your way, hit them in the back if you have the chance, and get out before they realize what happened. Are we clear?"

Lloyd was not very good at inspiring his troops, but at least his speeches didn't last for very long. The nine samurai nodded their heads in agreement before climbing onto their horses. Behind them stood twenty brave soldiers enlisted from the neighboring village for a slice of the pie. They literally wanted a piece of the pie: with the ravages of the war, towns had been pillaged, fields burned, and the residents had nothing to satisfy their hunger. The promise of a good meal was enough to entice many of them to join, but the shine of gold had convinced the rest.

Of course, they barely knew how to fight, knew nothing of the mission and had no idea they were about to attack a fortified camp—but they would provide a welcome distraction. By the time they understood, and tried to crawl away, they'd be hit in the back by many soldiers. Lloyd expected as much.

"We attack!" he shouted.

There was no impressive charge like in legends. The samurai moved slowly, partly to not attract any attention, but partly so their cannon fodder could easily keep up. They arrived at the outer fortifications unimpeded, as everyone assumed they were members of other units. After all, who would be crazy enough to attack a frontline army camp?

They passed soldiers in the middle of building the palisades and made it all the way to the officers' tents before two sentinels finally decided to ask what they were doing there. Even so, the sentinels approached unthreateningly with their lances down. One of them groaned, no doubt resenting any delay to him getting his meal.

"Stop there! What is your unit?" demanded the other.

Lloyd gave him a polite smile. His blade had barely left its sheath before the sentinel's head was flying through the air. The second watched its trajectory stupidly without even thinking to defend himself or raise the alarm, and suffered the same fate a second later.

Shouts began in the camp; the time for discretion was over and the samurai spurred on their horses. Behind them, the soldiers they'd forced into enlisting widened their eyes in terror, finally realizing their true mission. They shot in all directions to escape the camp before being killed, and in doing so, adding to the rising chaos.

"Remember! No heroism!" yelled Lloyd, nodding in the direction of the daimyo's tent.

The problem with Atsuko's disguise was that it kept her classed as an ashigaru. While Takeko and Ibuka could get out of the unpleasant jobs because of their noble birth, she was still obliged to carry out the camp duties despite her new status as a bodyguard.

"You could ask for me to stay with you to concentrate on my mission," she protested the first night.

"I could, but I won't," replied Takeko peaceably. "I've already asked an unknown soldier to defend the daimyo. I wouldn't dare to bring more attention on you by asking for more favors. Plus…"

"Plus…?"

"It builds character."

Atsuko thought her character was built just fine, thank you very much, and that digging in the latrines with a tiny spade was not about to change her fate.

She was wrong.

Because the spade in question was about to save her life.

She felt the vibrations of the marching of hooves before her brain even heard the sound, and she turned around, the spade raised. The swing of the sword that should have hit her head instead bounced off the tool in her hand and scraped her shoulder. Before she had the time to react, the rider was already long gone, headed in the direction of the daimyo's tent.

"Arm yourselves!" screamed a voice in the distance.

Atsuko dragged herself out of her state of shock and set off at a run towards the battle, her yari in hand. She wasted no time in wondering how many attackers there were or if she stood a chance; she burned with shame at not being at her daimyo's side when she had sworn to protect him. He might have been a pig, but it was a question of honor.

The attackers were well organized. They surrounded Kayano's tent from all sides and chopped any soldiers who got in their way into pieces. Taken by surprise, the defenders had no time to organize, were dispersed and out of formation, and some were unarmed and some were without armor, which made them easy targets.

Atsuko arrived at the tent the moment one of the samurai, a tall and thin man with a shaved head, ripped open the fabric with a swipe of his katana. She threw herself forwards to stop him, but as if by sixth sense, the warrior turned at the last second and blocked her yari.

"Well, well," said Yoshisada with a cruel laugh, "what do we have here?"

He put himself into *jodan*, a particularly aggressive defensive stance, and Atsuko understood he didn't take her seriously. All the same, she was disguised as a simple ashigaru—and probably more significantly—he had no desire to waste time. This misplaced self-confidence offered an undeniable advantage to the teenager.

Even in spite of that, she was almost impaled in the first second. Yoshisada was at least as skilled as he was arrogant.

In a dojo, the jodan stance helped achieve a large blow from high to low, putting all the weight of your body behind the hit; but Yoshisada changed direction in the middle of his swing to hit sideways. Atsuko didn't even see the swing but put up her yari on instinct. Her reflexes helped, but it was luck that saved her, which meant that the tip of the sword hit the metal part of the hilt. The strength of the blow knocked her back while the samurai adjusted his position in surprise.

"Not bad, kid. Nobody could normally survive my attack. Our boss told us not to waste time, but I can't let someone who saw my secret move stay alive. Sorry, nothing personal."

Atsuko grimaced and got back into the defensive stance. Her shoulder hurt, and she really wished she had her katana. With her weapon of choice, she might have held against this formidable warrior—maybe. But with a yari it was suicide. She used its length to try and keep Yoshisada a distance away, with little success. The samurai anticipated her feints, and he soon gained a look of disappointment.

"I thought you'd be better than this, but your little show there must have just been lucky. Ah well, goodbye, boy."

He moved back into jodan. Concentrating hard, Atsuko got ready to block the same blow and realized too late that this time that he was using a normal strike. She spun around, tripped in the fabric of her trousers, and felt the blade rip her tunic and scrape her skin. She fell backwards into the mud and the shock took her breath away as she dropped her weapon. She was alive, but for how much longer?

"Let's finish this. The others are waiting for me," said Yoshisada.

He raised his weapon—and then looked one last time at his opponent laying on the ground with their tunic ripped open. His eyes widened.

"A woman? You're a woman?"

Atsuko finally regained her breath. Her hands found the hilt of her yari and she used the confusion to swing sideways at her opponent from the floor. The samurai expected many things, but not that. Astounded to be fighting against a girl, he took a second too long to try and understand it and jumped back too late. The steel forcibly struck his shin, and he screamed, stepped back and lost his balance. Unlike her enemy, she didn't waste time talking to provoke him or congratulating herself—she took the chance to hit him again, wounding him in the arm, before pushing her yari into his torso with both hands. Yoshisada groaned like a dying animal, pushed his hands onto the hilt as if he could survive just by the strength in his arms—then his eyes clouded over, and he stopped moving.

Atsuko stayed down for a few heartbeats, covered in blood and her tunic in shreds. Her first instinct when she regained her senses was to adjust her belt to rearrange her tunic and cover her breasts again, like that was more important than the current situation.

Then, she got up, took Yoshisada's katana and headed in the direction of the battle.

Ibuka was very pleased with himself: thanks to his sister, he'd found himself in the best position in the army. Kayano might have a bad reputation, but he knew how to treat himself. The food was better than anywhere else, and the best thing was that this mission meant no real danger. If only this assignment could last until the first battlefield, Ibuka would be the happiest of men.

In the tent, the atmosphere was jovial, helped along by the couple of glasses of saké the daimyo had so generously served. Not enough to be drunk, but enough to raise morale and spice up the conversation.

"So how will you celebrate our victory?" asked one of the bodyguards, a jolly man with an impeccable moustache.

"I'm going to take a walk in the Imperial gardens in Edo," said Ibuka dreamily.

He was met with waves of laughter and he implored, "What? What did I say?"

"Nothing, nothing, it's normal, you're still young! You have such a reputation that we sometimes forget your age," chuckled the man with the moustache. "But seriously, who wants to celebrate a victory in a simple garden? What kind of company can you expect to meet among the bamboo and flowers?"

"Right!" confirmed the man next to him, the oldest among the group, and he flicked his remaining tuft of grey hair. "A victory should be celebrated with women, not with plants!"

"*But beautiful plants*," interrupted Kayano, teasing.

He was met with polite chuckles, and satisfied with his proven humor, the daimyo arranged himself more comfortably in his cushions.

"You absolutely must visit the pleasure quarter. You can't imagine what you haven't experienced yet," finished the mustached man.

The men all chortled while Ibuka, blushing deeply, tried desperately to find an escape. His eyes roved around the tent and landed on Takeko. Sat in a corner silently for over two hours, she was so unnoticed that everyone had forgotten she was there.

She met his gaze, always impassible, and he felt himself blush even more. This wasn't the type of conversation a woman should be listening to. Luckily his sister was outside, digging in the latrines…

It was a bit unfair, but no one had asked her to join the army, right? She had to live with her own choices.

That was what he was thinking when the screams started in the camp.

"What's happening?" asked Kayano, trying to jump up from his cushions.

The man with the mustache stuck his head out of the tent opening.

"I don't know, Master. Sounds like fighting."

"And what are you waiting for? Go check it out!"

Instead of a response, the samurai froze for a moment, until his legs and arms folded like a doll. His head rolled on the floor and stopped at Ibuka's feet, who looked at it with a rising horror. His mouth was dry and he did everything in his power to not piss here and now. He couldn't look away from the opaque eyes of the dead man, which stared at him accusatorily. A few seconds earlier the man was joking about girls and pleasure and now he'd never touch anyone again, wouldn't celebrate any more victories.

"Defend your daimyo!" wailed Kayano. "Defend your daimyo!"

Ibuka felt like he was trying to move through water. He put his hands on his katana but the simple act of unsheathing it seemed insurmountable. All around him, the other guards were acting with grace and professionalism—the man with the grey hair no longer seemed like an old man but had shifted into a seasoned killer.

That didn't stop him from falling within three hits, under the blows of an enemy samurai who laughed raucously while hitting him, as though he were possessed.

Ibuka finally managed to draw his sword and adopt the defensive stance. For now, the daimyo had his eyes closed and was reciting prayers to the kamis, but this moment wouldn't last. He had to react, he had pretend to do something. After all, this attack couldn't last long; reinforcements were surely already on the way and the assailants would have to fight them all to get out. All was not lost.

But Ibuka hadn't realized that the rest of the camp was paralyzed in fear, in spite of his hopes for rescue.

With a great effort of will, he managed to make his legs obey. In a move he hoped would not have to last long, he shifted to stand just in front of Kayano.

"Whoever dares to attack the daimyo must do it over my dead body," he announced with an air of bravado.

"That can be arranged, little boy," growled Nobusuke as he entered the tent.

10

The camp was complete chaos, and in the dimming light of sunset you couldn't tell friend from enemy. Atsuko sprinted towards the daimyo's tent, trying to get used to the balance of her new katana. Yoshisada was much bigger than she was, and you could tell from the larger hilt of the weapon; not a huge deal, but enough to make her adjust her usual grip.

The closest soldiers had abandoned their fortifications to intercept the intruders, but they had come across fleeing enemies and chased after them instead of tackling the ones that were left in the camp—the most dangerous ones. The teenager stifled a sob and sped up even more. If she got there too late, she could never forgive herself.

To her great shame, her thoughts didn't go first to the daimyo she swore to protect, but to her brother, and to Takeko. What would she do if something happened to them?

No. Impossible. Her mentor was unbeatable. And her brother… if only he wasn't affected by the events, if only he wasn't paralyzed in fear…

She arrived at the tent as Takeko sprung out of the opening, holding back the steel surrounding her with her naginata. Two samurai who were trying to get the better of her had to step back to avoid losing an arm.

"Not bad for a woman," growled Saizu trying to reassert his stance.

"Not bad for anyone," corrected Masajiro, righting himself to come back into *iajutsu* position. "Don't underestimate her because of her gender."

Normally, Atsuko would have appreciated such a comment; but this time it made these two men more dangerous. She herself had only survived the previous fight because her opponent had underestimated her and been surprised by the revelation of her true identity. She couldn't count on the same element of surprise again.

Without altering her course, she pointed her katana at Masajiro's back and prepared to run him through, but he blocked her with almost no effort, like her sword was a reed in the wind.

He didn't even bother to draw his weapon but instead followed her movement by pushing her lightly with his palm. Knocked off balance by her momentum she stumbled, almost falling over. At the last second, she managed to regain her balance and faced him snarling, furious at being so easily knocked off balance.

"Hey look, another woman," observed Masajiro with an amused chuckle. "In disguise this time."

"What are you talking about?" protested Saizu. "That's a man!"

"'They have eyes, but they do not see,'" Masajiro quoted with sentiment. "A Christian missionary taught me that."

"Tell me your life story later. Let's hurry up and cut these two bitches and get the Masamune."

Adding a movement to his words, he thrust and feinted in a low and short movement to force Takeko back. The maneuver would have succeeded against a less experienced warrior, but Takeko simply stepped out of the way without falling into the tent. She knew time was on her side.

"Your problem is that you insult those of the fairer sex," mocked Masajiro, getting ready to put himself back into position. "All because they don't give you a second glance and they prefer my seductive traits. Seriously, ladies, if you had to choose a partner out of us, which one would you prefer?"

He spoke in a harmless tone, and his easy smile could put any conversation partner at ease. Only a smirk at the edge of his lips betrayed him and broke his charm. Atsuko jumped back, and the sword that should have decapitated her only managed to cut off a chunk of her hair. All while still talking, the samurai regained his position with an inhuman speed—he was maybe even faster than Ibuka, which the young woman would have never thought possible. With her heart beating hard and sweaty palms, she got back into the defensive stance.

"You see, Saizu, she survived my attack. I told you not to underestimate her."

The Saizu in question didn't respond as he was too busy blocking Takeko's attacks. The young woman had moved onto the offensive and her naginata spun so quickly it blurred. She used its length to target his legs, then his head, then his torso, aiming the tip with a surgical precision and the hilt with brutality.

But her opponent was no easy target either. Even though he wasn't used to fighting against such a warrior, he still hadn't been hit. With his face scrunched up and his tongue out in concentration, he danced around Takeko, blocking all her attacks.

Unlike most others, he fought with a weapon in each hand, and his *wakizashi** blocked as if by magic, dodging the blows by a hair's breadth every time.

Then he stepped back, spun his weapons in the air and gave her a smile of satisfaction.

"You're good. But I can kill you," he finished.

* A curved Japanese sword similar to a *katana* but slightly smaller.

"Big mouth, small dick," she said, with the venom such an insult deserved.

Atsuko had been locking metal with Masajiro for twenty seconds, and neither could gain the advantage. Twenty seconds didn't seem like much, and it was the end of the world at the same time. After the duel against Yoshisada and the run through the camp, Atsuko couldn't catch her breath. She was starting to lose her concentration. In front of her, Masajiro was still as fresh as ever, still smiling, still charming.

"Magnificent!" he complimented when her counterattack forced him backwards. "Such flamboyant style!"

"Exceptional!" he commented when she blocked his strike. "I think I already know the answer, but are you sure you don't want to change sides? I'd be delighted to take you on as a student."

Atsuko gave no response, trying to save her breath, as she was slowly realizing that she wouldn't win this fight. He had an extra half-inch of reach, a microsecond of reflexes on her and she could not break the defenses of this man with the infectious smile. The reinforcements certainly weren't far behind, but while Masajiro was blocking her like this, she wasn't at the side of her daimyo and she had no idea what was happening in the tent. Maybe he was in the middle of being killed while she could do nothing about it.

She risked a glance towards the town curtain and almost had her throat slit by the sword of her opponent that missed her jugular by a fraction of an inch.

"Come now, don't underestimate me like that," preached the samurai. "It's a bad idea to take your eyes off your..."

He couldn't finish his sentence before Ibuka burst through the tent fabric, having been kicked violently from behind, and landed brutally on Masajiro's back. Masajiro fell forwards and with admirable reflexes, managed to stop his fall by putting out his hand. He avoided the worst, but his grip on his sword loosened.

Atsuko had won. Her adversary had no defense and she could decapitate him in one swoop. She met his eyes, and he gave her a rueful smile, as though he was apologizing that their fight had ended in such disappointment.

The young woman raised her katana and made a split-second decision. Instead of finishing the enemy on the ground, she spun around and hit Saizu in the back while he fought off a fresh assault from Takeko.

The blade pushed into his unguarded side, and his mouth opened in an 'O' of surprise as he fell silently, with no last words, with no insults.

Masajiro took advantage of the moment to get up. He spared a look at the body of his companion and then contemplated the two women advancing towards him, as well as Ibuka pathetically trying to get up off the ground.

"A gentleman knows when he's lost a fight. He also remembers who saved his life," he stated before launching himself backwards.

Takeko was expecting a last-ditch assault and put herself into the defensive stance. It cost her a precious second; in the time she could have pursued her enemy, he had already jumped on his horse and galloped towards freedom, cutting up any soldier who tried to stop him.

The samurai who'd kicked Ibuka came out of the tent.

Nobusuke had expected a difficult fight, but all the bodyguards of the daimyo were weak. He had beaten them effortlessly. His eyes lit up at the sight of the Masamune in the hands of the daimyo. Immediately, he had been tempted to seize the legendary katana for himself and flee to some isolated corner of the island where no one knew him.

Then Lloyd had come into the tent and all thought of treason dissipated like sand on the ground.

"Don't kill me," begged the daimyo, throwing himself to the ground. "I'll give you anything you want! Money, information—"

"It's your sword we want," replied the Templar.

"Yes, yes, of course! Here it is, here—"

Kayano was cut off; the Englishman split his skull at the forehead, scattering his brains all over the tent.

"I hate cowards," snarled Lloyd, stowing the Masamune. "How could he have held such a piece of art for so long?"

Then his gaze fell on Ibuka, shaking and curled up in a corner, his arms enveloping his whole body. Lloyd's disgust increased tenfold.

"And speaking of cowards, here's a fine specimen. My katana is dirty enough for today; Nobusuke, I'll leave you to deal with it."

The samurai nodded his head in obedience and raised his sword—but it was too easy, too disappointing. After being so close to getting the Masamune, Nobusuke needed to let off steam. He picked up the coward by the shoulders, turned him over and kicked him up the backside out of the tent hangings.

But as Nobusuke emerged to finish it, he came face to face with Takeko and Atsuko, both in a terrible mood.

The mission had gone perfectly. Less than three minutes had passed since the start of the operation and now it was time to fight to retreat. The daimyo was dead, the Masamune was in Lloyd's hands, and the Englishman could not be happier.

Outside, he saw Saizu's body, but that couldn't ruin his good mood. He had known in advance that there would be losses and that they were acceptable. Nobusuke was up against two opponents and seemed to be struggling, but again, it was of no matter. Regardless of whether he lived or died, the mission was a success.

Lloyd saw a horse tied up two paces away, its colors covered in dirt. If he could get in the saddle, he could escape the camp before the first shots. He headed towards the mount and saw the young coward from before in his way. With a blank expression, the boy trembled from every part of his body.

"I thought I told Nobusuke to finish you off," snarled the samurai.

Moving to the boy's side, he wanted to strike him with a vicious blow to the stomach, a blow that would expose his guts but would take time to empty him of blood and cause immeasurable suffering. Cowards didn't deserve a decent death.

The boy's katana blocked the strike as if by magic, and Lloyd's attack failed.

The Englishman frowned. What just happened?

Impatient to get on his horse, he increased his pace and struck again, this time with the real intention to kill. A tsuki to the throat, clean and efficient.

Once more, the katana blocked the attack, and the

blow missed its target. Once could be a coincidence. Twice required the reflexes and talents of one who usually didn't walk among mortals.

"Who are you?" asked Lloyd incredulously.

The boy didn't answer, too frightened to speak even one word. He held his sword in front of him with no energy and didn't even try to get into the defensive stance.

The Templar had practiced the way of the sword for long enough to know that a clear head was needed for a fight. Anger, hatred, and yes, fear, diminished your reflexes and anticipation skills. A tortured being like the one in front of him should not have been able to block his blows.

Unless he was even better when he wasn't completely terrified.

Lloyd blinked, suddenly interested. It had been a while since he felt the rush of his blood like this, that thrill of adrenaline that slowed time and sharpened his vision. He got himself in the *hasso** position, ready to use the move that had won him so many battles; a diagonal swipe that was so fast and powerful that even someone who had been expecting it couldn't block it. The young man in front of him had dilated pupils, pale skin and sweat dripping down his face. He was no threat; he looked like a rabbit being threatened by a lion.

* Offensive stance used in the katana disciplines.

However, the Templar didn't want to take any risks. He put all his strength into his attack, pushing from his back and legs. He was more muscular than most Japanese men and had already taken so many opponents by surprise as they tried to block, before realizing that they were already knocked back off balance.

The coward in front of him recoiled rhythmically, moving his blade around Lloyd's own with a devilish ease. For a fraction of a second, no more, Lloyd found himself exposed. If the enemy thrust forwards, he could hit him right in the heart.

But the boy returned to the defensive stance, still trembling. Lloyd realized that on one hand he'd met someone exceptional, and on the other hand that he didn't have the time to play with him. Soldiers were approaching from all sides to capture him, and were watching the fight with wide eyes and open mouths. Even amateur warriors could recognize a fight between grand masters.

"We'll see each other again someday, kid," whispered the Englishman. "In the meantime, try to toughen up."

He ran backwards, knocked down a soldier in his way and sliced another in two from the groin, and he used the break to grab the reins of the horse.

That was the moment that Atsuko chose to leap at his back with her katana raised. Blessed with a sixth sense, Lloyd blocked the attack and struck out with his left hand. He hit out with a tsuki to the throat that took her breath away.

She fell backwards, unable to catch her breath, and he took advantage of the moment to mount the horse.

One glance backwards confirmed what he already knew: Nobusuke hadn't survived the fight with his two opponents and his body lay on the ground. Acceptable losses, as he'd already expected. He spurred on his mount and headed towards the edge of the camp. Luckily, the fortifications weren't yet finished and confusion still reigned.

He grimaced as he saw soldiers armed with guns, but they took too long to understand what was happening and he was long gone by the time they'd aimed their shot. The first shot passed far away from him, the second barely went near him and the third went into the trees as he reached the relative safety of the forest.

He had won. Against an entire fortified camp, he'd won. Against a whole army, he'd won. The daimyo was dead, Musashi's Masamune was in his hands. The Templars would be pleased.

He put his hand to his back and his smile of victory turned into a snarl of fury.

In the confusion, he'd lost the Masamune.

Slowly, Ibuka came to his senses. He felt like he was in a nightmare and couldn't tell what was real or fake. Had he really fought? He remembered seeing a terrifying man looming above him and did what he could to survive, but his opponent had been so skilled. Even in total defensive stance, he'd almost been hit many times.

So this was battle? It was even scarier than the moment in the hills. There was so much death, so much blood. Whichever way he looked, all he could see was bodies.

Some of the bodies were the samurai that had attacked the camp but many more belonged to acquaintances, to friends, to allies.

"Atsuko," he rasped, suddenly remembering that his sister was here, too.

He had promised to protect her. He was so stupid! He couldn't even protect himself. If she was dead, how could he forgive himself? How could he tell his father?

"I'm here," replied a voice next to him.

He spun around, and sure enough, there she stood next to him, covered from head to toe in blood like a killer kami. Her voice was hoarse, her eyes were bulging, and she grimaced while she massaged her throat, but she was alive, and that was all that mattered.

"You're still a coward," she grumbled. "But this time at least you were useful. You managed to stall their leader's escape. And look at the result—look at what I managed to get back!"

Despite her pain, she managed a small victorious smile as she showed him the Masamune. She had managed to grab it from Lloyd when she jumped on his back, and as he was too preoccupied with his escape, he hadn't noticed its absence. She hadn't been able to protect the daimyo, but at least she'd retrieved the sword.

And according to Takeko, that was the most important thing.

Ibuka picked up the weapon with reverence and examined it.

"So, this is what they were after," he murmured. "To attack a whole army for this..."

He stopped himself as the shouts closed in around him. The Aizu daimyo finally arrived on the scene, accompanied by his elite soldiers and gunners ready to shoot.

"What happened here?" boomed Matsudaira Katamori.

He looked at the young man in front of him, arms crossed over his ceremonial armor.

"Shiba Ibuka, I'm counting on you to explain everything. Do not omit any details. Where is daimyo Kayano?"

Ibuka opened his mouth, then closed it again, incapable of forming a satisfactory response. What could he say? He had failed in every sense. Everyone had seen his cowardice. This time, he was finished. He'd be sent home in disgrace—if they didn't tell him to take his own life.

And then, someone shouted from behind him, one of the men who'd watched the fight:

"Ibuka was a hero! He stopped their leader by himself! It was a fight worthy of Musashi!"

"His katana was faster than the wind!" called another with shining eyes. "Ibuka didn't even strike back, he was happy humiliating his opponent and forcing him to flee!"

"Look at all the bodies of the samurai who died attacking the tent. Ibuka was amazing!"

"He got back the Masamune the enemy tried to steal," clamored another. "Look! He has it in his hands!"

Dazed, Ibuka looked around at all the soldiers who'd seen his fight against Lloyd. Next to him, his sister lowered her eyes, her expression indecipherable.

The young samurai kneeled before Katamori:

"Master, my behavior is inexcusable. I was tasked with the protection of daimyo Kayano and I failed. He died from the many blows of his attackers. I am ready to accept any punishment you deem appropriate."

The daimyo surveyed the battlefield filled with bodies, then the boy kneeling in front of him. A master was dead, and that was not something to take lightly. But Katamori was a fair man, and his voice trembled as he extended his hand to his hatamoto to help him get up.

"You fought against forces much stronger than yourself, and you made many victims, Shiba Ibuka. You succeeded in getting back the Masamune of Kayano's ancestors and you made the leader of his attackers flee. Nobody could have done more than you.

"Not only do I confirm that you cannot be blamed for the murder of the famous daimyo Kayano, I declare here and now that you acted as a hero. Your actions will be rewarded for their rightful value, in this life as in the next, if the gods are just. Rise, my friend, my brother in arms, and join me in my tent. We will honor Kayano's memory with those closest to him."

Ibuka rose incredulously. Next to him, Atsuko ground her teeth.

And Takeko wasn't happy either.

11

The map was magnificent, drawn by one of the most important artists of the court. He had made a symphony of color; the blues of the rivers and the darks greens of the forests all stood out while the brighter greens of the cultivated fields around the capital shone even more. Dragons spread their wings in the four corners and sea monsters populated the oceans.

But the most impressive thing was the figurines.

Each represented one unit and each one was different, sculpted by hand and in luxurious detail that bordered on the neurotic. A mini samurai spiritedly raised his katana, while another prepared to strike. There was a skinny lance wielder wearing oversized armor, a soldier reloading his rifle, an angry-faced officer shouting orders, a horseman spurring on his mount and a gunner loading a cannon.

But Emperor Mutsuhito was unmoved by this work of art. The only thing he saw was the imbalance of the armies in view. The enemy forces represented more than fifteen thousand men, while there were only five thousand Imperial soldiers. No level of detail in the figurines could hide that fact.

"Takamatsu, Aizu, Matsuyama, Kuwana… all traitors for following Tokugawa in his rebellion. How could I have been so blind for so long? I should have executed him while he still lived in Edo instead of banishing him and letting him gather his army."

"You would have turned him into a martyr, Your Grace," interceded Harry Parkes in a calm voice. "Some would have praised your firm hand, of course, but most of the daimyos would have wondered if they'd be next on the list. It likely would have caused a worse rebellion. At least Tokugawa showed his true nature. You can take him on in all serenity, with no fear of looking like an abusive Emperor."

"Take him on in all serenity?" repeated Mutsuhito as he flicked over the figurine of a samurai. "There are three times as many of them! They'll butcher us!"

"The power of an army is not only linked to its size," observed Parkes. "Alexander the Great took on the Persian army five times the size of his own at Gaugamela. And more recently, Marshal Davout beat the Prussians with only a third of their number. Even if I'm loathe to admire a Frenchman."

"Those two examples came to you so quickly because they're the exceptions," grumbled Mutsuhito. "Normally, such an imbalance in troop numbers is insurmountable."

"Don't underestimate yourself," replied Parkes. "The shogunate soldiers are mostly conscripts, peasants they've quickly given a lance or a weapon to. They're impressive in number, but I guarantee that most of them will retreat at the slightest trouble."

"We're not like your British citizens," protested Mutsuhito. "Fleeing in the face of the enemy is unacceptable—even our peasants have too much honor to compromise themselves in that way. They would rather be chopped into pieces than retreat."

"Then they'll die," said Parkes simply, while carefully cleaning his glasses. "What these little painted figurines don't show is the difference in experience or materials between the troops. Your allies Shoshu and Satsuma possess operational cannons and even Gatling machine guns that we supplied them with after training them to use them. I have the greatest respect for the sword talents of the samurai, but I'll always put my bets on the side with machine guns."

The Emperor frowned and examined the map once more. Parkes could not blame him; he was still young and had never seen the damage that well-placed artillery could cause with his own eyes. Of course, he'd heard stories—he'd been told all about the bombardment of the Japanese ports by Western ships, but it was one thing to hear about it and a very different thing to see it.

The truth was that the world was changing. Knights had dominated the European battlefields for centuries before the French defeat at Crécy proved that a longbow was far superior against plated armor. It was the same for the Japanese samurai: what use was a katana against a revolver, or worse, a machine gun? Their days were numbered.

As Tokugawa's troops would soon find out.

Parkes picked up a figurine of a samurai and gasped as the tip of a wakizashi cut him on the thumb. A drop of blood appeared, and Emperor Mutsuhito burst into childish laughter.

"Be careful, Consul. Our warriors are more dangerous than you think."

When Lloyd finally returned to Edo covered in dust from the journey, he was in a murderous mood. He wasn't used to failing his missions, and this one had been particularly crucial. Especially because the way in which he'd lost the Masamune was completely ridiculous. He could accept being killed in a fight, or having to retreat in the face of more numerous forces, but to admit to getting the sword stolen by a mere child without him realizing was beyond his possibilities.

Like seeing his blows blocked even though he'd struck to kill. Undoubtably, if the fight had lasted a few seconds longer, it would have ended in blood—but that was only a small consolation.

His rage must have shown on his face, because no one bothered Lloyd as he crossed Edo Castle to reach his lodgings. Parkes must still have been in a meeting with the Emperor and wouldn't call upon him until the next morning.

The moment he reached his office, a guard hurried towards him, wringing his hands.

"I must warn you..."

"At ease, soldier. The bad news can wait a few minutes. I'm desperate to take a bath and get rid of this dust from the road."

"But..."

He realized what the soldier was going to say when he saw a thin silhouette sitting in his armchair, and all thoughts of relaxation disappeared from his mind.

"You have a visitor," finished the guard feebly, lowering his head.

Lloyd waved him away impatiently and entered the office, closing the door behind him.

"I wasn't expecting you so early."

"And I wasn't expecting you so late," replied the other icily. "Do you have the Masamune?"

"There were complications."

"Aren't there always? But you didn't answer my question."

Lloyd never appreciated an interrogation. He believed in the Templars' ideas, in a perfect order that allowed for the progression of civilization on all continents—guided by a benevolent and paternal hand, of course. He was prepared to do anything for this vision to succeed, but that didn't stop him from occasionally having murderous thoughts whenever the hierarchy became too oppressive towards him. His guest had no doubt never fought for his life, as his talents were better suited to matters of intrigue and politics. But that didn't stop him from looking down on Lloyd, a man who could slice him in half in a heartbeat.

"No, I don't have the Masamune," snarled the British man, gritting his teeth. "But the daimyo Kayano is dead."

"Which doesn't really help our affairs," said the other, pointedly. "Kayano was a brute with no real power, and the loss of his precious sword would have been a fatal blow to him. Now he will be replaced by his successor, who might prove more capable."

"What does it matter? We killed his hatamoto, dispersed his soldiers. The Saigo domain will never recover."

"Even worse," said the man in the shadows. "Don't you get it, Lloyd? If you're right and their house is destroyed, they will no longer be capable of guarding Miyamoto's sword. It will be given to another daimyo, a more ambitious one, and it will be better guarded. We had the chance to get our hands on that artifact and you let it slip away. The masters of the Order will not be pleased."

If they're not pleased, why not let them head to the battlefield and see how well they do! Lloyd almost responded aloud, before regaining control of his emotions.

Once, the Templars had been great warriors unafraid to go on a crusade for their ideas. But lately, the Englishman had the impression they were wilting, like a blade left too long in a furnace. The more complacent they became in the comfort of their European fortresses, the more they lost sight of the real world.

Though Lloyd could be impulsive, he wasn't stupid, so he held his tongue.

"What are the Order's instructions?" was all he said.

The messenger smiled.

"All is not lost. The Emperor admires you and has many meetings with the consul. Tokugawa is removed from his post. Japan heads at full steam towards modernity. There is just one thing left to do to make up for the Masamune disaster."

"And that is?"

"Win this war and crush the Shogun's armies."

It was amazing how quickly routine was re-established. Atsuko had lived through the most terrifying night of her life, fought against adversaries who were more determined and skilled than any she'd faced before, saw men killed in front of her eyes, slipped in the blood of the daimyo whose life she'd sworn to protect… and yet nothing changed.

The next day, the army continued its march as though nothing had happened. Soldiers had removed the bodies, but no one had thought to clean the huge pools of blood that still lay on the ground, the last souvenir of the violence that invaded the camp the night before.

The only difference, in the end, was the soft spot for the ashigaru Mori Taisuke, which disappeared at the same time as the death of the daimyo, and she had been unceremoniously reintegrated into the regular troops—where she had to endure non-stop questions.

"So, what happened? The officers won't tell us what happened!"

"Is it true the camp was invaded?"

"They say there was over a hundred of them!"

"What did they want, exactly? They had no chance!"

"Did you fight?"

"How did you manage to survive?"

"Come on, admit it, were you scared? Did you piss yourself?"

"What about Shiba Ibuka? Is he as impressive as they say?"

"They say he fought against four by himself!"

"He decapitated one like this, *slitttt*, and then another, *slafff!*"

Atsuko had gritted her teeth, smiled politely and recounted what happened the best she could. When she mentioned that she'd finished off two samurai, they stared at her, commiserating, before nodding, *yeah, yeah*. She stopped trying—no one believed her, and it didn't really matter.

But the rumors that spread through the camp about her brother only served to annoy her. Of course, she had to admit that he'd looked impressive while blocking the attacks of that *gaijin*[*] like a demon, but once again, he hadn't mastered his fear or escaped his paralysis, and had been useless. Yet still, everyone admired him and thought he'd acted like a hero. His legend only grew, and his name was on everyone's lips.

The daimyo Matsudaira Katamori had reclaimed the Masamune and now wore it on his side. No one had contested his right to wear it, even though he insisted on meeting with Shogun Tokugawa for his blessing. He had no idea it had belonged to Musashi, but the simple fact that it was a Masamune made it precious enough. Katamori was no Kayano—he had real authority, more men, more status, and a better sense of tactics. No group of samurai would succeed in infiltrating the camp to take it from him.

[*] Japanese term for a foreigner.

Now that she had found her place in the army again, Atsuko rarely saw her brother; though she did spend time with Takeko, away from the watch of the others. The feat of meeting up with her without being spotted was one of her daily training exercises.

She became better and better at making up excuses for slipping away during breaks, passing through to the other side of the convoy and disappearing into nature. She who had once worried so much about peeing in private now blended into the background with supreme ease.

The training she had undergone in her youth had made her flexible, but Takeko insisted on making her more so, and during their conversations, the two women practiced bends that were increasingly difficult. The curving forms that were difficult for Atsuko were made more so by the daily training as much as the day's march.

"What do you think of your brother?" asked her mentor one night, on all fours as she wiped the sweat from her neck.

Taken aback by the question, the teenager took a moment to reply, and taking that as a response in itself, the other nodded her head.

"I see."

"No, that's not what I meant," she protested. "It's just that—it's complicated. He's brimming with talent, incredibly skilled. But besides that—"

"He doesn't have an ounce of bravery," finished Takeko before smiling at the surprise of the girl.

"What? I was there during the fight, remember? I saw him in action, or rather in inaction. If it was up to me alone, I would have told his commanders about his cowardice. But I held my tongue, and look how helpful it was for him: now he's become a living legend."

"Why did you ask me the question if you already knew what I thought?"

Takeko lay back with her arms crossed and contemplated the stars burning in the sky.

"Because you care for him in spite of everything, that much is clear. If not, you never would have joined the army. You dreamed of adventure, but you never would have taken the first step if it wasn't for him. In order for me to make the best use of you, I need to know your motivations, that's all."

"Best use of me?" Atsuko repeated, also lying down. "Is that all I am to you?"

Takeko cracked a smile.

"Do you want there to be more between us?"

"More? Like… oh," gasped the teenager, realizing what she must have implied. "Oh, no, no. Sorry, that's not what I meant. I just mean, it makes me feel like a tool, a weapon you just have to aim in the right direction."

"Shame," commented Takeko mildly, "that that wasn't what you meant. But yes, you are a tool, just like I am.

"We work for forces that are far beyond us and neither of us has the full picture. All we can ask for is to contribute to the peace and happiness of the Japanese people, and hope that our actions bring good consequences. Because every action has consequences. Just ask your brother."

Atsuko frowned.

"What do you mean?"

"He's become a demi-god to the others, thanks to actions he did not commit. You and I know that we killed those intruders, not him. And yet he's worshipped for it. But…"

"But what?"

"But that also fosters jealousy and boils the blood of young idiots who want their shot at glory. Watch your brother during the march tomorrow and you'll see what I mean."

"Watch my brother? But we're not in the same place in the column, how will I see him?"

"Exactly, that's your task for tomorrow. Get away to watch your brother without being seen. I leave the method of choice to you."

"In the middle of the march with all the sergeants watching? That's—"

"Impossible? Hardly, just a little complicated. And I watched you fight those samurai without flinching. What's a little sneaking around compared to that?"

12

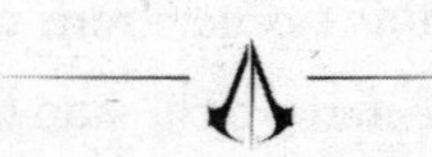

Atsuko thought for a long time about the best way to infiltrate the samurai, but the marching order was carved in stone and every soldier had their place in the column. If she tried to break ranks, she would be caught by a sergeant, and that was if she hadn't already been told on by her neighbors.

She had tried and re-tried Takeko's mission in every possible way and almost gave up—until the solution came to her at the end of the morning. It was simple, elegant, and unpredictable.

She took advantage of a break to approach the sergeant, and with the air of a beaten dog, pouted:

"Lady Takeko asked to see me. I bet they're going to interrogate me again about the attack on the daimyo."

"During the march? She can't wait for tonight at camp like everyone else? Who does she think she is?

"Just because she's the only female warrior, she thinks she can break the rules!"

"Yeah, exactly," replied Atsuko in a grave voice. "So, can I stay here? Can you cover for me?"

The sergeant glanced towards the front of the convoy. He wasn't stupid and knew exactly what would happen if he tried to defy a direct order from the young woman. Officially, he would be in the right, and his superiors would congratulate him for following army rules to the letter. Unofficially, his career would be down the toilet. He drew himself up to his full height like a cockerel showing off.

"Out of the question, Taisuke! You are a soldier, and as such must take responsibility for your actions! If you had defended the daimyo better, we wouldn't be in this situation! Go, find Lady Takeko, and hurry up. If you dawdle, I'll take you to her myself!"

Atsuko feigned horror and protested one last time to keep up the act, then quickened her pace and left her place to head for the front of the column. Some officers looked at her curiously, but their discipline was such that they all assumed her to be on a mission—otherwise why would she break rank like this, and why would her sergeant allow it?

Soon, the teenager arrived at Takeko's level, who frowned as she saw her approaching.

"What are you doing here?"

"I'm accomplishing my mission," Atsuko replied. "I am mixing among the samurai."

"With no disguise? Or subterfuge? How did you manage to leave your unit?"

"I told them you'd ordered me here to discuss the events leading to the death of the daimyo. So now it's all down to you."

"What? But why did you…?"

Takeko stopped herself and a rueful smile appeared on her face.

"Well played. I should have been clearer in my instructions, but in fact, this was one of the only solutions. Sometimes, there's no need for a disguise to blend into the masses."

Atsuko felt stupidly proud of the compliment. She cleared her throat to hide her embarrassment and then looked for her brother among the column of samurai with her eyes.

"You wanted me to come and watch Ibuka, right? What am I supposed to see?"

"You'll understand soon enough. He's very persistent."

"Who is?"

"Patience."

Takeko said no more, and the teenager felt herself losing said patience. Ibuka was in the middle of a small group of hatamoto and threw his head back in laughter while one of them told a joke. He seemed completely at ease, like he always did when at the center of attention.

And then she saw him tense up.

A samurai barely older than Ibuka pushed into the middle of the group, breaking up the conversation. The samurai might have been good-looking in his youth, but it seemed life had been hard on him and erased any appealing qualities. Smallpox had left his skin ravaged by pustules. In the middle of his face was lasting damage from a violent blow from a club or other blunt weapon, his nose was broken sideways, and he had several teeth missing. It gave him a particularly carnivorous smile, especially given his size. He was a head taller than Ibuka and had shoulders the same size as their father's, which was saying something.

From her distant position, Atsuko couldn't make out what the two samurai were discussing, but it didn't seem to be cordial.

"Who is he?" she asked, turning towards her mentor.

"Uesegi. A fine warrior, but he's also a brute with no morals or scruples. Normally the ugliness on the outside doesn't reflect the inner beauty, but in his case the two are the same."

"How did he become a hatamoto, then? I thought a sense of honor was a prerequisite."

"As I said, he's excellent with a katana. A lot can be forgiven for a genius, as you well know. People turn their heads to avoid looking at him at dinner, but that doesn't change his talent. Until your brother arrived, he was considered the great hope of daimyo Katamori. But now that they have someone who's just as skilled, but far more sociable, charming and presentable, Uesegi has been turned from shining star to skulking in the shadows. And he doesn't like that very much."

As Atsuko watched, Uesegi violently pushed Ibuka, who would have overbalanced and fallen to the floor if the others hadn't caught him. He got up in fury, as far as she could tell.

"Don't worry, it won't come to swords," said Takeko calmly. "This type of scene has been going on for three days and your brother has never risen to the bait, and we're all wondering why not. Out of fear, maybe?"

Atsuko didn't answer and gritted her teeth.

"For now, everyone watching is on his side," continued her mentor. "They believe that your brother is proving his honor by not sinking to Uesegi's level and that his resolve is an asset.

"But how many provocations will it take to change their minds? There's a fine line between resolve and cowardice. And we both know what happens in that case. The legend of your brother will fizzle out, seeds of doubt will be planted, and pressure will build until his total humiliation."

"Who's to say that isn't what I wish for?" countered the teenager. "That the truth comes to light."

Takeko stared at her for a long moment before her smile reappeared.

"No, you're not that kind of person. You want to protect your brother, no matter the cost. And in the current case, Uesegi is a threat."

"I couldn't exactly challenge him to a duel in my brother's place. That would have the opposite effect!"

"Yes, and not to mention that I'm not even sure you'd win the duel. Oh, don't get annoyed, I've seen you in action and you're very skilled, but Uesegi is—like I said, before your brother arrived, he was the best weapon in Aizu. Maybe you could win, but I don't want to bet my investment in you on a roll of the dice. However, if he were to suffer an accident..."

Atsuko turned to her mentor in shock.

"What are you trying to say?"

"Me? Nothing. Just that this Uesegi is a problem. I saw today that you can get creative. If ever you were to find a way to help your brother and prove to me your ingenuity, you'd be killing two birds with one stone."

"But..."

"I wish you could see your face!" smoothed Takeko. "Come on, you don't need to decide right now. Once more, I will intervene to help you. I have a mission for you, which means you both must leave the camp for a while. Time while Uesegi can't make any moves against Ibuka. And who knows, perhaps he'll come back covered in even more glory?"

"What are you plotting?" protested her student. "And why would my brother agree to help you?"

"Because if you refuse this mission, I'll tell everyone the real version of what happened during the attack on the daimyo," stated Takeko calmly while looking Ibuka in the eyes. "And to prove what I say is true, I will challenge you to a duel to the death. I could even accuse you of harassment. That would add a little spice to the story."

"You really think you could beat me? It would be your head rolling at my feet," growled the young man, meeting her eyes.

But even despite his threats, he was already deflating under her gaze like a balloon, and the spy let out a cruel laugh.

"You could beat me with one hand tied behind your back. But you don't have the heart to do it. You know it, I know it, and your sister knows it. And anyway, this mission is so important that I'm willing to risk my life for it. So, what will it be? You obey, and you can leave the camp, which will take you far from Uesegi, who's ruining your life. Or you defy me and your secret sees the light of day, which will push him to make your life even harder—not to mention my own blade."

For the first time, Atsuko felt a shiver down her spine. Since she'd met Takeko, she'd always admired the young woman, who lived life as she wanted with no fear of anything or anyone, without betraying her gender or her ambitions. But this was all just a façade. Behind her bright eyes hid the darkness of someone who did not hesitate to use blackmail or murder to advance her plans.

What had she gotten herself into? She looked at her brother and corrected herself: what had *they* gotten themselves into?

"Supposing I agree. I'm a hatamoto for daimyo Katamori. He won't like seeing me leaving on a mission for someone else."

"The daimyo owes me a favor and I have the perfect excuse: you are a legend, aren't you? Who better than you to carry out a dangerous mission?"

Ibuka gulped.

"A dangerous mission?"

"No, no, not at all. Forget what I said. So, if your daimyo accepts, are you in? I don't want to use force; I'd prefer you to accept gracefully."

"Of course," conceded Ibuka. He always conceded.

"What must we do?"

"Perfect," stated Takeko, finally relaxing a little. "You'll see, it's very simple. Our army has encircled Edo and we're now marching towards the south to meet up with our allies. If our information is correct, we might meet the enemy around Fushimi village, and we think that the enemy will get there first and set up camp."

She pulled a bottle out of her vest like the one daimyo Kayano had emptied every day—but the liquid inside of this one was much too dark to be saké.

"Atsuko, empty this into the town well. I don't need to tell you not to drink any of the water once you've completed your task. If we're right, this simple action could give us a decisive advantage during the war."

"And what about me?" Ibuka asked impatiently. "What do I have to do?"

Takeko gave him an icy glare and he met it without blinking. There was no love lost between the two of them. Maybe the blackmail hadn't helped.

"You… you will accompany your sister to her mission location, to ensure that she is not attacked on the way."

"I'm perfectly capable of defending myself," protested the concerned party.

"I have no doubt, but it's out of the ordinary. A woman alone who can fight with a katana or a yari, who isn't afraid of brigands—that will attract attention. And that's exactly what you want to avoid during an infiltration. The presence of your brother will give you a more credible story."

"So I'm just a—an accessory?" groaned Ibuka.

"Is that a problem? I thought you'd be happy you don't have to fight," replied the spy.

Ibuka closed his eyes in frustration while Atsuko was thinking quickly. Something didn't add up.

"Why us? The army has tens of experienced scouts who have spent their time getting to know the area. And I bet there are assassins and poisoners too. So why send us when we don't know the terrain?"

Takeko gave her an appreciative nod.

"Good point. For a start, the scouts are dependent on their daimyos while your loyalty, if I'm not mistaken, is wholly mine. And I'm not mistaken, am I?"

The brother and sister murmured *no, of course not*, and the young woman nodded in satisfaction.

"You see. Besides, this mission could turn dangerous; the scouts have many good qualities, but they are used to fleeing in the face of danger. I know that you're better armed and braver in the face of any problems. Or in any case, one of you is."

This time, Ibuka lowered his eyes and Atsuko felt a wave of fury. Not just against her brother, but against Takeko too, who happily provoked him at every chance. Fine, she herself wanted to mock him, but she had good reason, and she didn't want someone else to do it in her place.

"Alright, we get that we're your pawns," she grumbled. "And that you don't hold us in high regard. If we have to obey, we will, but I'd appreciate it if you stopped tormenting my brother like that."

"Oh, you have no idea just how highly I do regard you," replied Takeko without the slightest hint of emotion. "And that's exactly the reason I want you to accomplish this most vital mission: I want to see what you're capable of out in the world. If you come out of it with flying colors, I'll have a proposition for you."

13

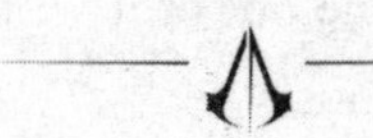

It was difficult to find clothes that were more uncomfortable than a uniform. For budgetary reasons, they were a standardized size, which meant that you often found yourself with boots that were too big, a tunic that was too tight and trousers that were too short. Not to mention the poor quality of the unbreathable fabric that held in sweat and caused terrible smells after a long march.

Even so, Atsuko was starting to miss her military outfit. The peasant clothes she'd had to put on smelt strongly of manure and urine and the scratchy wool rubbed her arms, while she could feel tiny insects running all over her skin. The only thing that stopped her from screaming and rolling on the ground was her brother's composure.

"How can you stay so calm?" she raged. "You lose all control against a katana, but you turn to stone with these bugs?"

"The insects in question aren't going to horrifically dismember me," said Ibuka, with a hint of his old smile. "It's just a bit uncomfortable. At least my fears are logical, little sister. I don't want to die before I'm twenty years old—that seems more rational to me."

"More cowardly, yeah," replied Atsuko while frantically scratching her left arm.

They moved forwards carrying a cart filled with bric-à-brac, as impressive as it was worthless. Broken plates sat next to rusty forks, dresses that had been eaten by mites, and half-rotten eggs. Takeko had taken a mean pleasure in gathering the most useless objects in the camp to throw into the cart.

"You are peddlers," she told them solemnly. "You travel from village to village to sell your wares."

"All the more reason to give us something useful," protested Atsuko, picking up the hilt of a broken lance. "None of this trash has any value!"

"We are at war," replied Takeko. "A cargo of any quality would attract suspicion. You are barefoot peddlers, so play your role until the end."

And that was how Atsuko found herself dragging a cart filled with trash through the middle of a muddy field.

Because of course it was raining, too.

"A coward maybe, but I'm still alive," remarked Ibuka. "If I'd acted bravely and honorably, I'd have been dead in daimyo Kayano's tent defending a pig who didn't deserve his title."

"Or you might have sliced up the enemies into pieces," countered the teenager. "I'd understand if you were a normal swordsman, but everyone says you're the most gifted of your generation."

"That wouldn't have mattered much against so many enemies. Especially because they were quite skilled themselves. No, little sister. If I had fought as honor requires, I'd be dead now—like all of Kayano's hatamoto. So, I prefer my cowardice, thank you very much."

Atsuko frowned; her brother had changed. Once, he'd been ashamed of his doubts and fears. Now he seemed almost at peace with himself. How could he so easily discuss such a humiliation?

The brother and sister saw the walls of Kyoto before the houses of Fushimi. The small village was located on the edge of the large city, a mixture of fields and tightly packed-in shacks.

The residents were victims of all the usual inconveniences of proximity to a large city, like the inflated markets, the arrogance of the nobles, and the weight of taxation without benefiting from it. The walls were too far away to protect them from wolves and the patrols were too scattered to discourage brigands.

But the residents didn't complain—what would be the point? They broke their backs and continued to cultivate the land like their parents and grandparents before them, hoping that those in power would continue to ignore them and gallop through, away from their homes.

The first person to see the fake peddlers was a young woman named Madoka. She put her hand to her face to better see against the setting sun, then cried out in joy and ran towards the center of the village.

"Merchants! There are merchants!"

The residents emerged from their houses, from the stables, and from the old windmill, their eyes full of hope. They were only a few steps away from the magnificent markets of Kyoto where the richest perfumes mixed with the most noble silks, but they knew full well that they were not welcome there and they could never afford the exorbitant prices. But the peddlers, on the other hand, would happily accept chickens or meat in exchange for their torn fabrics, and after all, who needed a luxurious dress to work in the fields?

Atsuko's heart skipped a beat when she heard the shouts by all the peasants. She cursed herself for not insisting on better quality merchandise from Takeko. How would they react when they saw the contents of the cart?

"How much for this pickaxe?" asked a man, picking up a half-broken tool.

"How much for this?" clamored another, examining a tunic with holes in.

It seemed that everything found a buyer if the price was right. And of course, it wasn't the merchandise the residents were most interested in, but news of the outside world.

"Where have you come from?" pressed the one who bought the pickaxe. "From Osaka? Did you see the armies marching?"

"They say they're coming this way, is that true?"

"Did the Shogun Tokugawa really betray the Emperor?"

"Not at all, he came to free him from the influence of the Shoshu and Satsuma clans!"

"Talk quieter, what will you do if one of the city guards hears you?"

"As if they'd come here. And I'm happy shouting out loud what we all think!"

In the cacophony of conversations, tens of hands pushed Ibuka and Atsuko towards the square at the center of the houses, where the village chief insisted on serving them a bowl of soup.

Used to military rations, the brother and sister didn't flinch at the tasteless bowl in which a piece of meat that could barely be called such floated. They knew the peasants would go without so they could eat, and they felt even more guilty.

"You've arrived at the perfect time," announced the

chief with an enormous, toothy grin. "Madoka and Keitaro are getting married the day after tomorrow. If you would do us the honor of staying a few days, you can join in the celebrations!"

"That's, um..." babbled Atsuko, taken by surprise. "We have to return to the road. If we stay too long in the same place, our business will suffer."

"Come, come, grant us the pleasure! There'll be songs, dancing, and an enormous fire of joy! Visitors will come from the surrounding villages! We're even going to slaughter a cow!"

The teenager salivated in spite of herself. It had been weeks since she'd had a good meal, and the promise of a feast was more tempting than she ever could have imagined. On the other side of the table, Madoka gave her a shy smile. She held the hand of another peasant, who must have been Keitaro. From time to time, the two looked at one another in awe, as though they could barely believe their luck. And they were right: they never would have been able to choose one another without the interference of their parents.

Atsuko took a moment to wonder if she would have fallen in love if she'd had her own choice. She'd never been interested in the boys in her area. They were too stupid, too clumsy.

"What do you say?" pressed the chief. "Will you stay?"

The siblings looked at each other. It was hard to refuse such an invitation; peddlers normally had no schedule for their journeys and would never refuse a night of warmth and a good meal.

"With pleasure," said Ibuka, finally. "We wouldn't miss it for the world."

"It's decided, then!" exclaimed the chief between spoonfuls of soup. "We can set you up with Haku. He's our blacksmith, and he's used to setting up beds in his workshop."

The same Haku inclined his head from the other side of the table. He was a giant, but he had the gentle smile of a child. Watching him plunge his fingers into his bowl and lick them in delight, Atsuko realized that he was a bit of a simpleton, but that didn't take away from his hospitality in the slightest.

The evening passed under a constant barrage of questions. The slightest rumor caused an incredible reaction in this cut-off village, and Ibuka delighted in captivating his audience with tales from the Aizu court.

The peasants had never met any of the characters in his stories, but they clung to all the adventures of all these lovers with a childlike fascination.

"—and when the husband came home, he found his wife quickly getting dressed while the butcher readjusted his kimono. And you know what she said to him? 'You're the one who told me to go find what I needed at the market!'"

Raucous laughter filled the common room, and even Atsuko couldn't hide a smile. Japanese society could be desperately strict about relations between the sexes, but tensions released in the jokes told around a table.

"There's the story of the woman who didn't know how to fish. When a man asked for her hand in marriage, he explained to her: 'At least with you, I'll never have to eat sushi,'"* tried Atsuko when it came to her turn.

Once again laughter filled the room and the teenager relaxed. She knew the peasants had a much harder life than hers; they would never have the time to train with a katana, too busy with tending the soil and looking after their animals and paying their taxes to their masters. But even so, in moments like this, she envied their freedom—even if it was relative.

The moon was full in the sky by the time they finally went to bed.

"Over here, over here," called Haku, as happy as a child showing off their den.

He was definitely a blacksmith, but if he'd had any real talent he would have left long ago to set up in Kyoto or in the capital. What he confidently called a workshop was no more than a hastily constructed shed in which an old anvil that no one else would have wanted sat proudly. Bits and pieces of

* The author apologizes for the terrible joke.

blades attested to failed efforts to make a katana, while a badly formed breastplate stood in the corner as the representation of the high point of his career. Haku would be here his whole life mending plows and straightening horseshoes.

"It's not big, but it's home," he announced proudly. "You can lie down here next to the fire, then you won't be cold. Hold on, I'll go get some logs."

"Let me help you," insisted Ibuka.

"No need, no need! You both relax!"

Indeed, the giant had no need of any help. He came back with several large logs of wood that he carried on his shoulder as though they weighed nothing and put them in front of the furnace.

"There's only one blanket for you both. Sorry, I don't have any more," Haku apologized. "If you need some water, the well is just in front of the house. And for the toilets, they're at the other end of the village. You have to walk a little, but at least we don't have the smell!"

He stopped for a moment, delighted to have continued the evening's conversation a little longer, then finally headed to his bedroom at the side of the workshop. Soon, his regular snores shook the walls.

"Should we wait an hour to make sure everyone's asleep before we carry out our mission?" whispered Ibuka.

Atsuko didn't answer. The young man turned to his sister and was surprised to see her face crumpled in anger.

"What's the matter? Did I say something wrong?"

"No, it's not you," murmured Atsuko. "It's just that..."

"Just what?"

"We've been told to poison the well to affect the Imperial troops who'll come this way. But what will happen to all these people? They'll surely drink the contaminated water. The village chief, the blacksmith who welcomed us into his home, Madoka and Keitaro who are about to get married—they'll all die if we succeed in our mission. I'm prepared to do a lot to help our Shogun, but I won't kill innocents. I refuse to put the poison in the well."

Ibuka's mouth opened in a perfect O shape.

"Huh? You can't do that! This is the mission Takeko gave us! It would be treason! And worse she'd expose your secret—our secret—to the whole camp!"

"I'll take that risk. Anyway, I have no choice: I can't do it. I can't kill sweet Haku who gave us a bed, or Madoka, or Keitaro, or all the others. I just can't do it. They're already victims of this war, caught between two sides, and I won't stab them in the back even more."

"Well, it would be poison."

"I was talking metaphorically."

"Metaphorically or not, I thought you would follow Takeko's orders to the letter. Ever since you met her, she's all you talk about. Takeko this, Takeko that. Wouldn't it bother you to disappoint her so badly?"

Atsuko hesitated a moment at this low blow, but she'd made her decision and she put on an expression of resolve.

"She'll surely understand my decision. Or at least I hope she will. Ibuka, she needs us just as much as we need her, or she wouldn't be training me the way she is. I know there is always collateral damage in war, I'm not stupid. But I don't have the stomach to be a killer of innocents."

She pulled her knees into her chest, and suddenly the room felt cold, despite the furnace close by.

"Isn't it better to sacrifice a hundred people to save thousands?" tried her brother again.

"Maybe it is," she admitted. "And my decision is probably selfish, but why should the weight of this act lie on my shoulders? The Shogun has thousands of supporters. Why is it up to me to kill these hundred people, and to have to live with it for the rest of my life?"

She looked Ibuka right in the eyes, trying to make him understand what she was feeling, the suffering it was causing her, the dilemma they'd put her in. And it worked. He looked away and let out a long sigh.

"Very well, little sister. In any case, you're the hero of this story: I'm just here so you don't get attacked on the way. Let's stay as peddlers a little longer, and we won't talk about this ever again."

Atsuko thought she would have trouble getting to sleep after making such a decision. But exhaustion took her, and she fell asleep right away, cuddled against her brother like when they were younger, when they were inseparable and agreed on everything.

14

The next day at dawn, the siblings were ready to leave. Atsuko put her hand to the bottle against her chest and muttered a quick prayer to her ancestors. Had she made the right decision?

Madoka's excited face running towards her served in convincing her she was right.

"Are you sure you won't stay for the wedding?" protested the young fiancée.

"Yes, we're getting really worried about the political events in the region," explained Atsuko gravely. "The war is coming here, and we don't want to find ourselves in the middle of a battlefield with our little cart. We'll try to warn the other villages around here…"

"… and earn a little by selling our merchandise," finished Ibuka next to her.

"Exactly. The best opportunities come in times of war. But I wish you a happy marriage, Madoka. You're lucky;

Keitaro seems like an exceptional man."

"He's not as good-looking as your brother, but I'll make do," whispered the young woman into Atsuko's ear before giving Ibuka a wistful but discreet look.

The teenager rolled her eyes—here was another good reason to leave as quickly as possible, before the samurai could break up a marriage before it had even been officiated.

She was getting ready to leave when the blacksmith ran after them, red and out of breath.

"Wait! Here! I have a gift for you."

Proud of himself, he dropped one of the knives with a bent blade that had been sitting in a corner of his workshop. No one would want it, but he could have used the material to make something else, all the same. For the price of the metal, it was quite valuable—at least for the peddlers they were supposed to be.

"We can't accept," protested Atsuko. "As a matter of fact, we're the ones who should be giving you presents. You let us stay during the night. There's no need! Oh, I know, wait!"

She rummaged in the bric-à-brac and pulled out a tunic that was ripped on the side, but still usable.

"Here you go. Thanks again, Haku."

The blacksmith held the tunic against his chest as though they'd given him a kimono worthy of the Emperor.

"This is the first time anyone's ever given me a present," he gasped in wonder. "May the ancestors protect you on your journeys! May the onis stay away from your path!"

The brother and sister left the village waving their hands, their hearts warmed by the kindness of its residents.

"You see, Ibuka, and you were willing to kill all these poor souls just to get an advantage in the war?" asked Atsuko, more and more sure of her decision. "I'm sure Takeko will understand my decision."

"Let's hope so," replied Ibuka. "Let's hope so."

The peddler disguises were useful twice more as they crossed patrols, but soon enough, they came face to face with the Shogun's scouts. While they'd been on their mission, the army had advanced at the same time, before establishing an entrenched camp on a hill that overlooked the region.

"Sorry, we don't have anything against you, but you can't come in," said a soldier when he saw their peddler disguises. "The kamis know we need more clothes…"

"And saké! Definitely more saké!" added another.

"…and saké," admitted the scout. "But we're under strict orders: no civilian is to get within half a league of the camp."

"Excellent. But I'm no civilian," said Ibuka as he pushed back his cap to reveal his face.

He was well-known enough that the soldiers immediately bowed. Atsuko felt the typical wave of jealousy; she was the one who always did everything, yet he was always the one praised. While the soldiers bowed, she wondered how she was going to explain her actions in the village and justify why she hadn't poisoned the well. All she could hope was that her valor would be enough to justify this blatant refusal of a direct order.

Takeko once again did not meet them in her quarters, but rather directed them away from watching eyes, into a tent that looked like all the other soldiers' tents but didn't belong to anyone. There were cot beds inside and clothes hung up as though a unit slept there, and a quick glance would have dissuaded anyone from investigating further. But Atsuko, with her nose that had been desensitized in the army, immediately knew that something was suspicious: there was no smell of sweat.

"No one will disturb us in here," said Takeko, taking a seat on one of the beds. "Good. You're both alive, and that's already a victory in itself. Tell me what happened. Was the mission a success? I imagine it didn't cause you any problems, but I prefer to be sure. After all, how difficult can it be to empty a bottle into an unguarded well?"

"Well speaking of—um," babbled Atsuko. "I wanted to tell you that—"

"The mission went well," interrupted Ibuka.

Atsuko turned towards her brother, but he wouldn't look her in the eyes.

"What?" she said.

"My sister was amazing. While I kept the villagers busy, she poured the bottle into the well. There's no doubt the scouts who'll come here to drink will perish within three days."

"Excellent," said Takeko. "In that case, I can only congratulate you on a successful mission. I'll leave you alone so you can enjoy a few days of rest. Use it wisely, as it won't be long before we go into battle, and the first fight will already be decisive."

She got up gracefully, saluted them as equals, and then confirmed no one was watching the tent before slipping outside.

The brother and sister stayed alone inside, under a heavy silence. Atsuko was the one to break it:

"You're taking a big risk by lying to Takeko."

"Atsuko—" whispered Ibuka.

"I mean, eventually she'll realize we didn't poison the well. She's happy for the moment, but when she finds out, she'll be furious."

"Atsuko..."

"We'd be better off being honest and telling her the truth now. Honesty will pay off in the end. You can even say it was me that decided not to do it, since that's what happened."

"Atsuko, I really did poison the well," said Ibuka in a slightly raised voice to cut off her monologue.

Atsuko looked at her brother incredulously. Then she rifled in her vest and brought out the vial of poison, still full to the brim. She checked the stopper, and it was still sealed.

"That's not possible. What are you talking about?"

Ibuka was still refusing to look at her.

"Takeko had her doubts that you'd have the courage to kill innocent villagers. After we discussed the mission, she came to find me in my tent. She gave me a vial too and told me to use it if I felt you were hesitant. And you were. So, while you were asleep, I got up and poisoned the well."

To prove what he was saying, he withdrew an identical bottle to the one Atsuko carried and let it roll on the ground. It was completely empty. But Atsuko didn't need proof; she could feel the sincerity in her brother's voice.

"The courage?" she repeated slowly. "The *courage*? Really? You're the one telling me about courage? You—you knew—and she knew it too—and you both manipulated me!"

"Atsuko—" tried her brother again, as though he could calm her just by repeating her name.

"It's not just me you hurt. What about Madoka, who looked at you in such admiration? Or Haku, who gave us one of the only knives he owned? Or Keitaro? Or the others who cooked for us while they were living in poverty? You're telling me that—"

She closed her eyes, her heart beating violently. It had taken them three days to get back to the allied camp.

Everyone she just mentioned was probably already dead.

She fell to the side and vomited on one of the fake beds, emptying the contents of her stomach until all that was left was bile, and even so, she continued to vomit until she collapsed onto her side, exhausted, depressed, and with her eyes filled with tears.

"How could you—how could you—how could you?" she kept repeating.

"It was the best possible solution, and you know it," explained her brother. "And plus, you realized it yourself."

"*Me?* When did I recognize what it was to be, you murdering piece of crap?"

"You lamented that the decision fell on your shoulders. You should be grateful someone else reacted in your place. You don't have to feel guilty. The weight is on my shoulders."

Atsuko got up and wiped the spit from the edges of her lips and looked at him as though seeing him for the first time.

"Of course I feel guilty. Guilty for trusting Takeko. Guilty of having you for a brother. How could I have been so stupid? What am I doing here, exactly? I'm playing at being a soldier while you're getting along just fine by yourself. All you have to do is your usual: nothing at all. Except occasionally *killing a few innocents.*"

She spat those last words in his face and burst out of the tent in fury, without bothering to check her surroundings like Takeko had. It didn't matter anymore. Nothing mattered anymore. She didn't know how her life would continue, but it wouldn't be like this. She had to get out of there, and she'd find a purpose for her life later.

She marched in a rage towards the entry to the camp and when a sentinel asked her—asked him—what he was doing, she had an answer prepared. She had been perfectly trained, after all, to lie, to hide, and apparently to kill.

"Daimyo Katamori is sending me on reconnaissance."

"You'll have to tell him it's not possible, my boy," said the soldier, without moving to open the gate.

Strange. Normally the mere mention of his name was enough to push anyone to cooperate.

"It was a direct order from him," she insisted, bringing herself up to her full height.

"And my orders come directly from the Shogun. No one enters or leaves the camp. The enemy army is in sight."

15

Jules Brunet was not the happiest of men.

On the bright side, Tokugawa had chosen the best possible place for a battlefield. The Shogun's troops were more numerous but much less well-equipped than the enemy. The solution was therefore to find a position to impede the enemy artillery to maximum effect: a forest, hills, or even a village whose houses offered shelter against bullets and machine gun fire. In hand-to-hand combat, the samurai were capable of miracles—but you had to let them get close enough.

Furthermore, almost two hundred enemy soldiers were in no state to fight thanks to symptoms of a shocking illness. It seemed as though someone had poisoned one of the wells along the way. That gave Tokugawa's troops even more of an advantage in number.

But that was where the good news stopped.

The shogunal forces didn't have much of anything, particularly munitions. France had delivered a number of guns, but they were no use without any bullets or gunpowder. Reserves were so low that soldiers hadn't even been allowed to train with live weaponry. Most of them seemed happy enough to march under their sergeant's orders with a gun slung over their shoulder, and upon seeing the target dummies, cry out "Bang!" to simulate a shot. It was nice for morale, but the soldiers were wholly unprepared for a fight.

"We've got empty guns while the other side are deploying Gatlings," Brunet sighed, looking at the map.

Besides all that, the Shogun Tokugawa had come down with a high fever. Most thought it might be food poisoning, but those closest to him couldn't help wondering if it was the work of an enemy shinobi. In any case, the Shogun would not be well enough to lead his troops, which was a disaster. Even though Tokugawa wasn't a warrior, his presence alone would have been enough to spur on his soldiers. Brunet worried about the rumors circulating around the camp, doubting their leader's illness.

"Do you think he's actually ill, or just pretending to be so he doesn't have to go to the front lines?"

"I'd like to be in the infirmary just before a battle, too. Ouch, ouch! My skull hurts! I need to be examined!"

"Oww for me—it's my stomach, I think it's serious!"

Plus, the British navy had applied pressure on the port of Osaka by bringing its ships closer to the harbor, which meant the Shogun had to leave a section of his troops there. Even though Britain wouldn't partake directly in the war, their alliance with the Emperor was clear.

"Just like ours with the shogunate," murmured Brunet.

The only difference was that Britain had been much faster to prepare for battle.

And now, Japan's fate would be decided in one massive fight, just outside two tiny towns.

Toba and Fushimi.

Atsuko wanted no more to do with her brother and Takeko. She no longer benefited from any free passes and found herself once more among the ashigaru. The sergeant looked at her in her masculine disguise as though seeing her for the first time.

"Mori Kyosuke, was that it?"

"Mori Taisuke," corrected the teenager.

"Kyosuke, Taisuke, I don't care either way. The only thing I care about is that you've been a damn opportunist who left behind his origins and his comrades, too busy consorting with the nobility.

"You think you can just pretend like all that didn't happen? While we were building the fences, you spent your time trying to seduce Lady Takeko and getting chummy with the samurai. Did you really think you were on the same level as them? The truth is that they don't give a damn about you. You entertained them for a minute, but now that war is here, you find yourself back in the same position, with the same ill-fitting armor that we all have and the same yari to defend yourself with. The only difference is that you didn't bother to take the time to train with us and that will be your downfall. You didn't bother to get to know those who'll be fighting next to you, and you'll put our entire formation in danger."

"But—" protested Atsuko.

It was so unfair! So, she wasn't worth anything unless she'd spent time with her unit, was that it?

Was that it? She bit her lip as her actions over the past month came back to her. Okay, sometimes she'd been the victim of events beyond her control, but she'd also jumped at every chance to get away from the ashigaru at meals, to get sent on other missions, or even to sleep in a bed away from them. It was no surprise everyone thought of her as an opportunist: in a certain way, that was exactly what she was.

"You will therefore not be a part of our formation. I haven't been able to judge you in action and I don't want you to flee at the last second. You will be on our left flank, and your mission will be to deal with any enemies that make it through our defense. Is that clear?"

"Very clear," murmured the teenager.

In a way, it wasn't such a bad thing.

Instead of being squashed against other sweaty bodies that pushed you into hitting blindly forwards, she'd have more space to fight and twirl her lance like Takeko had taught her.

In deathly silence, she took her place in the column and awaited the order to march.

The hardest thing, in the end, was the waiting. She was ready to fight to the death, even against better-armed and better-trained soldiers, but with each passing minute she felt her motivation, morale, and enthusiasm sapping away. The feeling of fear rose in her stomach.

The samurai were the first to leave the camp, so handsome and dignified on their horses. Atsuko saw Ibuka trying to catch her eye, but she looked away. She wasn't ready to forgive him, not so quickly.

Then she saw her father and her heart skipped a beat. She'd done everything she could to avoid him these last weeks, and destiny had listened. He was as impressive as ever, with his huge shoulders and hands capable of crushing an enemy without even unsheathing his katana. She muttered a prayer that he would survive the battle and lowered her head to be sure he wouldn't recognize her.

And then it was her group's turn to advance. The sergeant barked an order and the ashigaru set off as one man. The soldiers talked amongst themselves, joking and worrying, thinking of their families, but no one said a word to Atsuko.

A light fog hung in the air, as though the ghosts of the ancestors were readying to march into battle beside them. In the distance, the enemy looked like ants, thousands of insects moving to get into position. From time to time, the boom of a cannon could be heard as a gunner tried to judge the best distance and angle. The most worrying thing about that was that the sounds didn't all come from the same place, so the Shogun's armies couldn't proceed in any direction.

A look to her left reassured Atsuko. An entire company of gunners stood there, with weapons ready to fire and their faces impassible. They had the advantage of the high ground, and it would mean carnage for the enemy troops if they attempted to climb the hill.

"Alright, men! Squeeze your ass cheeks, grit your teeth, and cross everything you can cross—it's almost our moment of glory!" screamed the sergeant. "We'll show these Satsuma and Shoshu pansies the cost of going up against us, and we'll free the Emperor from their influence once and for all! Don't try and play the hero! If we each kill just one of them, that's already enough, because we outnumber them! So, no reason it shouldn't go our way. Don't panic and protect your comrades. Understood?"

"Sir, yes, sir!" replied the ashigaru chorus.

Despite this show of confidence, they all had sweaty palms and looked nervously around them. Without armor worthy of the name, and on the front line, they would suffer terrible losses from the first blows—whether their side won the battle or not, some of them wouldn't return to their tents tonight.

Atsuko strained her neck to try and spot her brother or Takeko. The first was somewhere in the middle of the left wing, probably leading the attack. Ah! How nice for him. She had no more desire to help him; he'd chosen his own fate. The second was chatting with a state head with an insolent smile on her face. Atsuko bared her teeth—to think she'd idolized this woman—but she'd lied to her, she'd manipulated her!

Her train of thought was interrupted when orders fed back through the lines of command. The units advanced slowly, ready to charge down the hill.

The ashigaru moved on their turn, trying to keep rhythm even though the legs of some moved faster than others. Atsuko's mouth was dry and she suddenly needed to pee.

"First battle, huh?" chuckled a veteran as he saw her strained look. "Don't worry, we've all been there. If you want some advice, piss on your victims when you have a minute. Not only to calm your bladder, but it does wonders for your fear."

"Piss on my victims," repeated Atsuko through a grimace. "I'll try to remember that."

In the chaos of the march, she was separated from the soldier as he slowed his pace to reassure another recruit, probably to give him the same excellent advice.

And then the time for questions was over. Soldiers were streaming out of the woods in front of her, guns on their shoulders. The guns created a cloud of smoke while the ashigaru fell by the dozen. She felt a bullet brush her shoulder before exploding the skull of the warrior behind her.

"Keep going!" screamed the sergeant, miraculously unhurt. "Keep going! If you stop, you're dead!"

He was right; if they stopped, the guns could hit them much easier than a moving target. But that required a bravery bordering on madness, since knowing that continuing to charge meant another bullet was always waiting for them.

To the credit of the ashigaru, they didn't hesitate for a moment and continued to run, climbing over the bodies of their comrades. Atsuko followed them with her heart in her mouth and her head tucked into her shoulders. It was one thing to die in a duel at sundown, but it was an entirely different matter to die from a stray bullet when the battle had hardly begun. There was nothing honorable in it, nothing glorious, just the cold of the abyss and being forgotten in a nameless tomb.

Once more, the guns rained death down on the group. The most impressive thing at this distance was the noise. Atsuko had never seen firing weapons up close, and she hadn't expected the booming noise that covered their cries.

The veteran who'd reassured her fell just in front on her and she caught her foot on his body, lost her balance, and fell onto all fours in the grass before jumping up in the same movement and continuing the charge.

The Imperial soldiers were preparing for a new wave by the time she finally reached close range. She must have looked like a savage beast, her lips curled, her teeth bared, and her face covered in blood. The tip of her yari pushed into her first enemy with no resistance; he was still focused on aiming and fell in one blow.

She pulled out her weapon and traced a trail, then spun it and shoved the flat side into the throat of another enemy on the other side. While he desperately tried to regain his breath through a crushed windpipe, she chopped down the legs of a third and jumped into the fray where she collided with an officer, who seemed very surprised to find himself already in a melee.

"Come on!" she screamed. "Avenge the dead!"

Her ears rung and she thought no one could hear her, but her comrades took up her battle cry without hesitation.

"Avenge the dead!"

"Avenge the dead!"

"Avenge the dead!"

The ashigaru had paid a heavy price. They were terrified, they were furious, and they were ready to take out their feelings on someone. The Imperial soldiers tried to re-close their ranks, but they suffered from the opposite problem as the shogunal forces: they had been too well trained with the guns and poured all their confidence into them. Instead of pulling out a dagger to defend themselves, they tried to reload, with little success.

Atsuko took a moment to wipe the sweat dripping into her eyes and blurring her vision. It was only when she saw her hands that she realized it was blood. Luckily, it wasn't hers—or at least, she hoped it wasn't.

At the start, she'd tried to practice her martial art, using both the hilt and tip of her yari to spread devastation around her. But she soon returned to basics out of exhaustion: hit them in the stomach, pull out the blade before it hit bone, start again.

And then, with one blow, the morale of the Imperials was broken. The gunners started to flee, first one, then two, then a hundred. The ashigaru let out victory cries and set off in pursuit after them, mercilessly butchering any who turned their backs while their sergeants desperately tried to re-establish order.

Atsuko's head spun. She took a deep breath to clear her mind and finally looked around her. It was the first time she could see how the battle was going for the other units.

And her heart stopped. It was a disaster.

Her wing had only come up against the auxiliary troops. Meanwhile, the elite Imperial soldiers had attacked the samurai from both sides. Now that she took the time to listen, she could hear the booms of the Gatlings, which felled the warriors like wheat, no matter their talent in combat.

"Ibuka," she whispered in horror.

Then much louder:

"Ibuka!"

She had thought she wanted no more to do with her brother, but she was wrong. One betrayal couldn't erase their blood ties and all the years they'd shared. She hated him for what he'd done, judged him for his flaws, but that didn't stop her wanting to keep him alive, no matter what. The very thought of him in agony on the ground filled her with an unbearable pain.

She broke rank without hesitating and ran in the direction of the skirmish in front of her. On the way, she came across a unit of Shogun gunners and felt a glimmer of hope. The Imperial soldiers had turned their backs. If the gunners came forward just a hundred steps, they could cause widespread death.

"Follow me!" she screamed with no more consideration for rank or unit. "Hit them in the back!"

She was impressive, covered in that much blood. In the spur of the moment, she hoped that some would listen to her. But the gunner closest to her only laughed.

"Hit them in the backs? How? We don't have any munitions."

"What?" croaked Atsuko.

"The munitions didn't arrive in time," he explained

patiently. "All of our guns are empty and useless. Our only job is to guard the flank by giving off an impressive air, so the enemies think they're outgunned."

Now it was Atsuko's turn to laugh, with a trace of hysteria. Her brother and her mentor had compromised themselves to poison enemy troops, all to get an advantage in battle… and it all came down to nothing because of poorly prepared logistics. With no munitions, the Shogun's soldiers had no chance.

She glanced across the battlefield; she was no great strategist, but she knew enough to realize that the battle was lost. Despite a much larger numerical superiority, the allied forces were retreating from all sides. Lances and katanas were no match for the machine guns and cannons.

"Ibuka!" she repeated to herself.

She abandoned the useless gunners and ran to where the samurai were being killed. To their credit, they'd put up an impressive fight, but bravery wasn't enough. Faithful to their honor until the end, they'd all been blown to pieces rather than retreating.

No—not all of them. From the corner of her eye, she noticed one who'd broken away and run to hide behind a tree. She didn't even need to see the long, dark hair and the athletic build to know it was her brother. Of course.

It was a miracle he lasted this long without fleeing; he'd probably been too exposed to make a run for it.

She should have been angry at him, but the most important thing was the almost inhuman relief that coursed through her. He was alive!

Then she saw another samurai set off to pursue him and her blood froze over.

It was Uesegi.

16

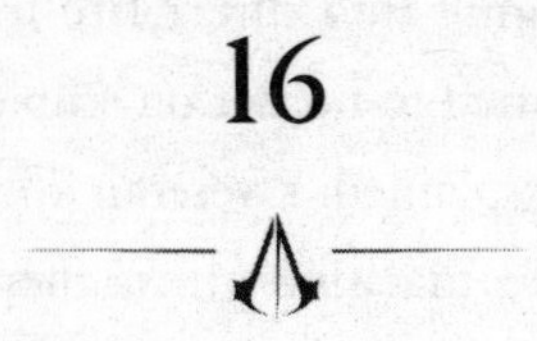

Ibuka couldn't understand how he was still alive.

He'd mounted his horse along with the others, a smile plastered on his face, repeating to himself over and over that it would be just like in training.

But that wasn't true; in training there wasn't this smell of excitement mixed with urine, and the air wasn't heavy with gunpowder.

All around him the other samurai were laughing and clapping each other on the back like children.

"Finally! I was starting to get bored!"

"We'll teach them a hard lesson!"

"Satsuma's warriors are all cowards anyway; they'll flee as soon as they see us coming!"

Some were even making jokes:

"Hey, do you know if Shoshu's samurai are good at pleasing women? Who knows, because you can only see them from behind! They're always running away!"

Ibuka was in no mood to laugh. It was his first battle, and he was probably much worse at strategy than the others, but even so, charging into direct fire from cannons and machine guns seemed to border on stupidity.

"It's logical," explained a veteran to his right. "If we don't take out the machine guns, they'll massacre our army."

Yes, it was logical. Someone had to make the guns unusable for the shogun to have any chance. But why did it have to be his unit?

"But we'll be more useful on the battlefield. Why aren't the ashigaru charging first?"

"Because they'd be blown to pieces before they'd even get close, that's why!" His neighbor chuckled. "They don't have our training or our armor!"

Ibuka struggled to see what half an inch of metal and years of practice with a katana would do to save him from the bullets, but he knew he couldn't retreat. Not anymore.

So he clung to the reins of his horse and desperately tried to fight the terror that overwhelmed him, and he awaited the daimyo's signal.

The signal came much sooner than he would have liked, and he charged alongside the others, hundreds of samurai from the five clans, all united in a common cause. In the space of a moment, his fear disappeared and was replaced with the certainty of victory. Who could go up against such power? Who could see them without wanting to flee? Who could...?

The first machine gun began firing and everything became worse than his worst nightmares. Men fell from left to right. He had trained with some of them for weeks; he'd asked one what they'd do when the war was over, and the one whose skull exploded in front of Ibuka had shown him an old portrait of his wife and children just the day before, and now they were dead within a few seconds.

He ducked his head against the onslaught and miraculously didn't get hit by any bullets. Unable to believe his luck, Ibuka briefly considered fleeing into the forest, but the surviving samurai continued the charge, pulling him along in a current he could not escape.

"For Tokugawa!" screamed a samurai in front of him.

Tokugawa, he must be joking. He wasn't even here; a coincidental illness had forced him to remain in bed. Ibuka would have done the same, but the *bushido* code of honor obliged him to fight to the death even if he wasn't able to stand. That was the difference between the Shogun and the samurai.

Eventually, the horses collided with the first line of enemies. With his eyes half closed and terror threatening to overtake him at any moment, Ibuka fought like a beautiful demon. Even in his current state, he was still a brilliant swordsman, and men fell one after the other all around him.

Then another round of machine gun fire began, bringing down more than thirty samurai on the first sweep. The enemies that had just hesitated now shouted out in triumph and sprung forwards, determined to make up for that hesitation.

Ibuka cried out as a naginata chopped off the legs of his horse. The horse fell and flung him forwards, where he had to roll to the side to avoid being sliced by a katana. He blocked the attack out of instinct, and the dismembered hand of his opponent dropped bloodily into the grass.

The man who'd joked about Shoshu's samurai fell from a bullet to the chest, and at last Ibuka glimpsed an opening in the shogunal formation. He didn't hesitate for a single second and sprinted towards the forest, towards freedom.

He no longer cared what it looked like. It wasn't cowardly to flee a fight that was lost before it even begun—it was pure pragmatism. To stay wouldn't be brave; it would just be stupid.

Repeating those words over and over to himself, he ran to the forest, expecting every second to be hit in the back by a bullet or hear the whoosh of an arrow, or the pounding of horses' hooves.

But it never came.

He made it to the edge of the forest, gasping for air and sweating beneath his breastplate, then threw himself in the welcoming shadow of the trees.

He didn't notice the huge silhouette following behind him.

Atsuko unbuckled the belt of her breastplate and dropped her armor onto the ground to gain some speed. Her brother was no longer visible, and Uesegi, after one last hateful glare into the forest, started to return very slowly to the battlefield. He raised an eyebrow as he saw her approaching at a sprint and raised his katana before lowering it once he saw the colors she wore.

"What are you doing here?" he demanded, sparing a glance towards the left wing. "Are we winning, or is the left wing in chaos? Well, talk!"

Of course, he thought she was bringing a message; there was no other reason for her to break rank like this.

"We're holding, but our losses have been awful," she responded. "I have to find your officer to give a more detailed report. What about your side?"

"We're being cut into pieces," growled Uesegi, "and the rats are jumping ship. That's what you can add to your report. The glorious hero everyone was counting on is nothing but a coward and a deserter. If we ever get out of this, I swear on the kamis that his reputation won't survive. Make sure to give his name to your superiors if they ask. Tell them that Shiba

Ibuka, golden child of legend and supposed future Musashi, fled with his tail between his legs."

Atsuko grimaced. Everything he said was true, and she would never have expected how much it hurt her. After the betrayal in the village, she thought she'd manage to cut herself off from her brother—but it wasn't true.

If Uesegi survived the battle, if he revealed what he'd seen, it wasn't just Ibuka who'd suffer the consequences. The Shiba name would be dragged through the mud.

"I'll tell them," she promised.

The powerful samurai was the only one who'd seen her brother flee; the others had been too busy with their enemies. Which meant…

She turned as if to leave, and then quickly spun on her heel and stabbed toward his stomach, prepared to eliminate the only witness to her brother's cowardice.

Against any opponent, the advantage of surprise should have let her win with this first blow. But Uesegi was not just any opponent. He possessed reflexes that were almost as refined as Ibuka's, and his body moved out of the way before he'd even realized what was happening. He couldn't completely dodge the attack, but the blow that should have impaled him only managed to slice his left side.

"What the hell are you doing?" he growled before his eyes lit up with rage. "Traitor!"

His wound was serious but not fatal. If Atsuko fled now, he'd find a way to survive, so she raised her lance in an act of defiance, hoping that the amount of blood he was losing might weaken him. Without that disadvantage, she'd have no chance against Uesegi.

Her train of thought was interrupted when the samurai charged at her. She thought he might have acted carefully, defensively, to wait and see what Atsuko would do. That's what Ibuka would do in the dojo.

But they weren't in the dojo, she wasn't going up against her brother, and Uesegi was more arrogant than any enemy she'd faced before. He didn't harbor the slightest hesitation towards her, nor the slightest doubt of his assured victory.

Atsuko blocked the strike with the hilt of her lance, deflecting the blow enough that the wood didn't shatter. The second attack whooshed past her head when she threw herself to the ground and then rolled over to avoid the successive blows.

"What's this way to fight?" raged Uesegi. "Stop dancing!"

"Easy for you to say when you've got a katana," replied Atsuko, taking another two steps backwards.

The only advantage to the yari was its length, and it wouldn't make much of a difference if she stayed on the defensive. She twirled her lance before striking three deadly blows to the throat, heart, and groin.

The samurai had never fought against a lance expert; most of the time, they were only used by peasants whose only training was to hit in rhythm and hit in the stomach, so he was almost surprised by the third attack.

Almost.

Swordsmen of Uesegi and Ibuka's caliber only came along once a generation in a town. They achieved this level of talent thanks to rigorous training and incredible reflexes, but also to an intuition bordering on the mystical. So, after Uesegi dodged the first two blows, he turned to the side to protect his injured side and the attack that should have caught his lower stomach only brushed his armor.

"Hey! Where did you learn to fight like that?"

"I could tell you, but then I'd have to kill you," snarled the teenager.

"You hold up well, I must admit. But here's the proof that a yari is nothing against a katana."

He got back into the defensive stance and executed a few wide blows with no grace or technique—or so it seemed, but all were targeted to be fatal. He pushed with so much strength that the young woman couldn't block, and swung with so much speed that she couldn't escape. She could only step backwards and backwards, and backwards some more, one step after the other, praying she did not trip over a branch or a hidden rock.

"A lance can only hit in the stomach. A katana can *also* hit in the stomach," explained Uesegi with a cruel smile.

Suddenly, in the middle of his assault, he lunged and she fell backwards, landing heavily in the grass.

"And so concludes the lesson," he said, raising his katana.

That was when the mortar shell hit.

Atsuko opened her eyes. She didn't remember closing them. Her ears rung and she felt nearly deafened. Her vision was blurred, and she thought her eyes were injured before she realized she was crying hot tears. A heavy smoke surrounded her, and the air smelled of gunpowder.

She weakly got to her feet while the world spun around her, and she had no idea which way was which. Her yari shone on the ground and she carefully picked it up to use as a crutch.

Her clothes were torn on the left side and her skin was lightly burned—nothing life-threatening, but it was extremely painful. Atsuko wobbled forwards a step, then another, before tripping on something and falling forwards. Her balance was completely changed.

And then she saw what had made her trip. She screamed, a scream that she barely heard through her shattered eardrums.

The shell had hit at Uesegi's feet and reduced his body to a soup in which his face still floated, fixed in an expression of shock. All his talent meant nothing against bad luck and a mortar shell.

Atsuko got up again, her heart in her mouth, and frantically tried to wipe away the entrails wrapped around her. She was alive and he was not, and that was all that should matter. No one else saw her brother flee—he'd survive, and so would his reputation.

The smoke dissipated and she surveyed the battlefield around her with one eye squinting. All over, the shogunal forces were fleeing.

Despite inferior numbers, the Emperor had won.

The only good news of the day was that the Imperial soldiers were exhausted, too. Instead of pursuing those who fled, they remained in position to take care of their dead and injured, which allowed their enemies to regroup farther away.

Atsuko stared at the body laid out on a stretcher in front of her and wondered why she wasn't crying. Her tears wouldn't come, as though she had moved far beyond this state of sadness, as if her heart had dried up.

Her father seemed small in death—older, too. He was missing his left hand, a hand that he'd used to support her throughout her childhood and adolescence, the hand that used to brush her hair.

Like most of the samurai, he'd died from a bullet, and somehow that was a comfort to Atsuko; no warrior came close to the powerful Shiba Tanomo. It had taken a coward with a gun to put an end to his incredible life.

"I only thought of Ibuka," she whispered, caressing his swollen face. "During the fight, I only thought about my brother. I saved him, you know. He's still alive. But you… I didn't even try to help you."

Her voice wavered, and the tears finally came.

"At the same time, there was nothing I could have done for you. You were in the heart of the fight, as always. You didn't run. You didn't turn your back to them. The bullet hit you from the front, right in the heart. I'm so proud of you, but what will I do now? What will I do without you?"

"You could join our Brotherhood," said a familiar voice behind her.

Once, Atsuko would have leapt up to salute Lady Takeko—but the battle hadn't changed her anger towards the young woman. She still felt used and had no wish to see the spy again. Not to mention, this was a moment of privacy. What kind of monster would interrupt her while she was saying her goodbyes?

"I hope you're happy," she snarled. "It was really worth it to poison the well in that village; thanks to that, we came away with a great victory. Oh, wait, sorry: we were butchered. And my father paid the price."

"I'm sorry about your father. Truly, I am. I didn't know him well, but no one had a bad word to say about him, and that means a lot, these days," placated Takeko, taking a seat next to her. "And as for the poison... not every Imperial soldier was going to drink from the same well. We took maybe a hundred, two hundred, soldiers out of action. If they'd been on the battlefield, the damage would have been even worse."

"Took them out of action?" Atsuko repeated. "It must be nice to live in a world where our actions don't kill anyone. The village residents aren't dead either, just out of action. You know, two of them were getting married? Madoka and Keitaro. Their names will haunt me my whole life, even though I didn't spill the poison."

"Saori," replied the spy, her eyes glazing over.

"Excuse me?"

"Saori. That's the name of the first innocent I had to kill. She was a servant in a castle I infiltrated when I was only sixteen. She was probably about the same age, maybe a little older. She surprised me as I was sneaking into her master's bedroom and she opened her mouth to scream. I put my hand over her mouth and tried to calm her down, but she fought me, and she was strong enough to get out of my grip. So I slit her throat."

Silence fell once more between the two women. Finally, Atsuko muttered:

"I'm sorry. That must be a hard burden to carry."

"Her only crime was to be in the wrong place at the wrong time. And for that, she died. And she's not the only one, Atsuko. From a very young age, they trained me in martial arts, calligraphy, and poetry. I could have had a normal life, but *they* decided otherwise."

"But who are *they*?" replied Atsuko. "And why all this mystery? If you want me to trust you, you have to realize it goes both ways! Perhaps I'd have gone through with my mission if I'd known who I was working for!"

The faces of Madoka and Haku appeared in her mind and she added in a small voice:

"... or maybe not."

Takeko looked around to make sure no one could listen in. They were very much alone, but she lowered her voice all the same.

"Very well. I follow the orders of a group named the Assassins."

"*The Assassins?*" repeated Atsuko doubtfully. "That's not very original."

"I know what you mean," said the spy with a smile. "But they're the ones who invented the term. Believe it or not, at the time, it was original. Do you know where the word 'assassin' comes from?"

The teenager shook her head and Takeko continued:

"How to best explain it? There is a community of men and women who've fought from the shadows since the dawn of time. Their creed is to promote peace between men by championing free will."

"The what for the what?"

"Overall, they believe that all governments end up corrupt and that the more powerful they become, the more harmful they become. They think of all humans as equals, irrespective of sex, religion, race, or birth. They consider a burakumin to have the same value as a samurai, and that the Emperor's reign had no legitimacy—and also that women have the right to choose their profession. You can see why their ideology attracted me."

Atsuko shook her head. It was completely ridiculous. The burakumin were pariahs, the daimyos ran their regions, and it hadn't changed in centuries.

But it was also a very appealing belief, incredibly attractive. Choose her own profession? To join the army without having to hide? Not having to stupidly wait for a husband?

"It's a nice dream," she whispered. "But a dream all the same. Society won't evolve so easily."

"You're right," admitted Takeko. "I don't know whether you've heard about the French Revolution. France is a country far away in the West that was ruled over by a monarch. And the citizens rose up to overthrow him. Years of conflict, bloodshed and suffering followed, and the kings even returned from exile—but in the end, France won its own liberty. The biggest changes come with blood, and the Assassins are there to help spill it."

"You said they invented the word," murmured Atsuko.

"The first killers in the Brotherhood used a lot of hashish, a drug that blurs the senses, so they didn't feel fear on their missions. They called them the *hashishin* and the word evolved over time to become *assassin*. There—now you know everything. You know who I work for, and who you could have worked for, if you wanted."

Atsuko bit her lip, lost in thought. She felt like a weight had just been dropped on her shoulders, one that was far too heavy for her to bear.

"I do want the world to change," she admitted after a moment. "I want to choose my own path in the world, and I want others to be able to do the same. But I don't know if I'm willing to kill an entire village for it. A village whose residents did nothing wrong, who welcomed us with kindness, offered us their hospitality and invited us to their wedding—a village whose residents are now all dead, because of you and my brother."

A new spark of fury ignited in her but dimmed quickly from a lack of fuel. Takeko's words were appealing and supported what Ibuka had said: sacrificing a few for the benefit of all. Wasn't that a good idea?

"I understand," replied Takeko. "Our path is not the easiest, and not everyone can take it. But you are an extremely promising recruit: brilliant, efficient, and skilled in improvisation, disguise, and combat. Would you allow me to continue training you? This war needs people like us. And I promise you that the next missions I send you on won't produce any innocent victims."

Atsuko took a moment to consider. Her father was dead. Her brother was—somewhere, but still just as cowardly, still just as hateable.

What did she have left to lose?

She nodded her head.

17

Matsudaira Katamori gazed out of the window of Aizu Castle, fascinated by the snowflakes beginning to cover the surrounding fields. Snow in October—now, that was something unusual at this latitude.

It was a magnificent sight—and a disastrous one. The wheat harvests would be complicated this year, and there would be a threat of famine the year after.

The daimyo let out a strained laugh. That would no doubt be another master's problem. In a month, two at most, he'd surely be dead in combat or forced to abdicate. So why worry about next year's crop?

After the Toba—Fushimi disaster, the year had only brought failure upon failure for the shogunate troops.

Tokugawa was too timid to openly defy the Emperor and was still desperately seeking a peaceful solution. While he waited, his allies were being slaughtered on one battlefield after another.

Osaka Castle had fallen in a single fight once its defenders realized the Shogun had fled from it during the night. Then it was Utsunomiya Castle's turn to fall, and finally, Edo's. The Emperor left Kyoto completely unchallenged to return to his palace.

Katamori had hoped that the relative isolation of Aizu would dissuade the Imperial troops from coming for vengeance, especially as autumn was nearing, but the enemies hadn't hesitated in marching north and flattened his defenses in Bonari, thereby opening the way into his domain.

And now, Aizu Castle was surrounded. It was only a matter of days before he fell, if he didn't find a way out quickly.

Atsuko remained in the steaming bath for a long time to guarantee her skin didn't carry any smells that could alert the guard dogs or give away her presence. She couldn't help but give a disappointed smile as she approached the fire that warmed the room. It had been weeks since she'd been able to wash, and while she was finally clean, she wouldn't stay that way for long.

She plunged her hands into the ashes and pulled out blackened chunks of coal, which she rubbed it all over her like the women in the capital did with their beauty products. Her face soon disappeared into darkness and only the hint of her white teeth stood out against her skin.

She ignored her usual clothes and rummaged through the large bag that sat in the corner of the room.

Takeko waited for her outside the room. She looked her up and down with an approving gasp.

"Perfect!"

"Oh, don't be so flattering," protested Atsuko. "Anyone can rub coal on their face!"

"Yes, but not everyone would be brave enough to do what you're about to do tonight. It's an essential mission—and as you wished, you won't have to deal with any innocents. The army besieging us is the enemy."

"What is it I have to do again?" asked Atsuko.

She knew the mission by heart, but her mentor's calm voice soothed her. Takeko had now been training her, as much as she could, for six months, and Atsuko had made great progress in all areas the Assassins seemed to expect of their members. She had learnt to disappear into the background, disguise her voice, to use all sorts of potions and to climb almost-smooth walls.

"To infiltrate the main camp and retrieve the battle plans of the Imperial army," answered Takeko as though it were the simplest thing in the world. "If you succeed, you will become a real member of our Brotherhood."

Atsuko nodded her head and saluted her mentor one last time before departing. She headed down from the first floor and located the rope where Takeko had left it earlier. She lowered it out of the window and slid down to the moat.

It was horribly cold—by the kamis, it had snowed this afternoon!—and the water was half-frozen, but she didn't cry out or let her teeth chatter. She bravely swam to the other bank with her bag held above her head to keep it dry and reached the other side in silence.

"You can't go by the drawbridge," Takeko had explained. "That's where the enemy will have the most lookouts. You must cross the moat. Good luck!"

"'*Good luck*,'" muttered Atsuko under her breath, too quiet for anyone to hear. "I'll give you good luck!"

She slid behind a bush and undressed completely, leaving her clothes crumpled on the ground. As naked as the day she was born, she opened the bag and took out new, dry clothes. They were good quality—and most importantly, they were jet black, to disappear into the night.

She completed her disguise by pulling on a pair of dark gloves, and her hands disappeared into darkness along with the rest of her. She wrapped her feet in two layers of fabric and tested the result along the bank using heavy steps. The fabric softened the noise, and she couldn't even hear herself moving when she closed her eyes.

Now the serious work could begin. With her heart racing, she moved into the streets of Aizu, completely empty of its residents.

She had lived here her whole life, and the town was normally full of people at all hours, even at night: there'd be people meandering from tavern to tavern, voyagers arriving after sundown, teenagers meeting in secret away from their parents. It made it even more painful to see the empty boutiques, abandoned homes, and shutters that clacked in the wind.

From afar, the Imperial camp was difficult to discern. The soldiers had not wanted to shelter in the houses for fear of an ambush, so they'd built their own fortifications all around Aizu. Hundreds of campfires reflected the moonlight from the ground, as though the plains were ablaze.

Just like she'd been taught, Atsuko scurried through the tall grass with all her senses on high alert.

A recent lesson from Takeko came to mind.

Only amateurs crawl on all fours. You might think it makes us more difficult to catch, but if anyone saw us, we'd be easy targets and we'd lose precious seconds readying to fight. A real Assassin always moves standing—but hunched over.

So, Atsuko moved forwards but hunched over, her hand on the sheath of her tantō. It wasn't physically demanding, but the stress still made her heart race and exhausted her as though she'd just completed a day's march. She eventually began to make out individual campfires rather than a full landscape of fire.

If she were in command of the camp, where would she have placed the sentinels? Atsuko quickly identified the most logical places that would allow for maximum possible perimeter view and ability to call for backup. It wasn't easy to think of everything, but some seemed obvious, like this dead tree stump that gave a wide view of the surrounding field while also offering protection from any attackers.

Atsuko withdrew her tantō. She had prepared for everything, even greasing the sheath so the blade wouldn't scrape against the leather, and the knife slid out without the slightest sound.

Once you're in range of your target, then and only then, do you crawl.

The teenager dropped to the ground, her nose to the dirt. The earthy smell remained strong as she propelled herself forward with her legs and elbows, staying as discreet as possible. She only raised her head at the last moment, her darkened face invisible in the dark.

She hadn't been wrong: there was indeed a guard sat on the tree stump. On a regular night's watch, he likely would have been alert to every noise, his lance raised and ready to spring into action to take on the threat or raise the alarm. But the enemies were holed up in the castle with a drawbridge as the only way in or out, and their scouts had seen no movement of troops. So the female guard was more relaxed—frankly, she even seemed a little bored. She'd leant her lance against the tree stump, removed the helmet that was crushing her skull, and was currently fighting the urge to fall asleep.

Satisfied, Atsuko retraced her steps and disappeared back into the grass where she could watch the movements around the tree stump. She just had to wait for the guard changeover; if the Imperial soldiers followed the same rules as those of the daimyo, guard duty lasted no longer than two hours to prevent tiredness and complacency.

She'd settled in for a long wait, but she must've been lucky in her timing; the relieving guard appeared much faster than she'd expected—only ten minutes after she hid. The soldiers exchanged a few words, and then the first left to get some sleep while the other took over the post.

Atsuko waited another five long minutes to guarantee the first guard was definitely gone before she resumed her crawling advance towards the tree stump.

Choose your moment to get up very carefully. Too soon, and your enemy will have time to sound the alarm before you reach them. Too late, and you might be spotted while you're still on the ground, which will put you in a very uncomfortable situation. A lot of what follows will depend on that first decision.

Atsuko moved forwards, inch by inch. Every one of her movements was already as slow as possible. Sweat dripped from her neck onto her clavicle and the tall grass tickled her stomach, threatening to break her concentration.

The soldier in front of her couldn't have been more than twenty years old. He scratched his hairless chin, yawned, and turned to put down his lance. That was the moment she chose to attack. In two strides, Atsuko reached the unfortunate boy and held the blade of her tantō to his throat.

"Just one word or one sound and you're dead," she whispered in his ear.

This was the most dangerous moment of her infiltration. Takeko had warned her: some want to play the hero at the first spark of action and stupidly try to fight and disarm their attacker or to warn the camp.

If that's the case, don't hesitate to slit their throat. Or the entire mission will be jeopardized, not to mention your own life.

Atsuko's hand tightened on the knife, but the guard had no desire to die for the measly wage he received each month—and that was even if they paid it on time. He slowly raised his hands to signal surrender. The stress made him gulp and his Adam's apple wobbled against the blade, at risk of drawing blood.

"Don't kill me," he whispered. "I have a wife—Madoka—she's pregnant—please don't let me die now."

The face of Madoka from the village sprung into Atsuko's mind. She lifted the tantō away a fraction but suppressed the attached emotions. If she failed, many more Aizu soldiers would die, soldiers who also had wives and children. It all came down to the same choice—was she right to have not poisoned the well?

"Come with me. Quietly. Slowly."

She led him towards the bushes, and he let her without complaint.

He experienced one final hesitation when Atsuko pushed him towards the edge of the forest. She could understand: over there, no one would come to his aid. But it wasn't as though he had a choice. She held the knife to his throat with more insistence, a drop of blood formed, and he continued walking with no further protests.

Once the trees closed in around them, Atsuko reached out with her free hand and unbuckled the guard's belt. The dagger he wore in addition to his lance fell to the floor, and she kicked it away to lose it in the leaves.

"I'm slowly going to remove my weapon," stated Atsuko in her most threatening voice. "Make no mistake, I'm completely capable of gutting you like a pig if you make the slightest suspicious move."

"I believe you," the boy hurried to agree, his legs trembling.

Atsuko had a hard time holding in a nervous smile. *Gut him like pig?* Where had that come from? The words had just appeared to her out of nowhere. She stepped back, still holding her tantō raised and ready to strike.

"What do you want?" stammered the sentinel. "If you let me go, I won't tell anyone I saw you."

Without daring to move too much, he pointed to his coin purse that had fallen with his belt.

"I'm not rich, but I received my wages two weeks ago and I—I was saving up to buy my wife a present. You can take it all if you want, but please don't kill me."

He was trying to make her feel guilty, and it was working. Atsuko felt a wave of compassion—before it was replaced by cold fury. How dare he put her in such a position? He was the enemy, and that was all that mattered.

"Silence," she snarled. "I don't want your money. All I want is information."

"Information?" the soldier repeated in surprise. "But I… I'm just an ashigaru; do you really think the generals share any of their information with me?"

"I know. That's why I need to know where the generals and the quartermaster have pitched their tent."

The young man's eyes widened, and he took a step back, but the threat of the knife brought him back to his senses.

"You're crazy! Why do you want to know that?"

"As I said, I need information. And as you pointed out, the officers are the ones who have it. So hurry up and tell me before I find a more cooperative sentinel."

The guard had no choice. He wanted to live, and he hurried to spill everything he knew. He didn't even try to lie;

the icy glare of his attacker made him suspect that wasn't a very wise idea.

While he talked, Atsuko formed a mental map of the camp in her head. The two armies had near-identical structures and followed the same strategy manuals. She'd thought as much, but she hadn't wanted to take the risk.

"Very good. When are you supposed to be relieved?"

"In… in ten minutes," replied the sentinel.

He'd answered too quickly—far too quickly, avoiding her eyes—and Atsuko decided he was lying. No general would change guards so soon.

"Very well. Let's see whether you're telling the truth. We'll wait ten minutes and see if another guard comes to relieve you at the tree stump. If it's true, he'll raise the alarm and I'll have to escape. If not—well, that means you lied to me, and I don't appreciate liars. Then I'll be only too happy to slit your throat."

She raised her tantō and the young man cowered.

"Wait, wait! I must have been confused. Relief won't come for another hour and a half."

"That's better," she said. "Now get undressed."

"Pardon?" babbled the guard.

"You can take off your clothes yourself or I can rip them from your corpse. Which do you prefer?"

Trembling, the soldier did as she said. He removed his tunic bearing the Emperor's crest, his breastplate, and after some encouragement from his attacker, took off his boots and trousers. He stood in his undergarments in the autumn cold, and his shivers now had more to do with the chill than his fear.

"Well done," said Atsuko, bending to pick up the rope she'd kept with her. "Go stand against that tree."

"You want to tie me up?" he whined, affronted.

"A minute ago, you thought I was going to kill you. That's progress, don't you think?"

"But—the wolves—the cold—"

"Your comrades will find you soon enough. Which would you prefer: running the risk of wolves, or dying here and now with a blade through your intestines?"

Put that way, the choice was simple. The guard leaned against the bark of the tree and let himself be tied with no further complaints. Once her task was completed, Atsuko shed her own clothes in three quick moves and went to pick up the ones the guard had left on the floor.

"Wait, you—you're... a woman?" gasped the soldier in complete shock.

"Finally noticed," said Atsuko. "Was it the breasts that gave me away?"

With an experienced hand, she tightened the buckles of the breastplate. The Imperial army was no better dressed than those of the Shogun and the uniforms were all provided in the same size. The armor swamped her slightly, but no one would notice.

She gathered her hair into the helmet and picked up the belt from the ground. Finally, she layered her original dark clothes on top. There was no sense in drawing attention before she got to the edge of the camp.

"I can't believe it," said the soldier. "When I tell the others I was bested by a girl, I'll be the laughingstock of all my friends."

"No need to tell them the truth," she suggested, patting him on the cheek. "Make up tens of scary seven-foot-tall masculine attackers."

On that note, she left her naked victim attached to the tree and set off for the Imperial camp.

18

Atsuko used the same techniques as before to approach the border of the camp. She returned to the tree stump, waited a moment to check no one had sounded the alarm, then moved directly towards the fortifications.

As she had expected, the discipline was weaker here than in the allied camp, and she was able to slip inside without a single sentinel noticing her dark form that blended into the night. As long as she stayed away from the torches and the campfires, she was virtually invisible.

Once inside the camp, she hid behind a tent and removed her black tunic. Now dressed as an Imperial soldier, she continued her advance without hiding, instead acting as though she had every right to be there. She'd learned this essential lesson the day Takeko had asked her to slip into the head of the marching column: once past the initial security measures, people usually acted on the assumption that you were supposed to be there and paid you no mind.

Atsuko headed towards the place the sentinel had mentioned, but even without his instructions, she would have known to aim for the tents made from rich fabrics that stood higher than the others and twice as big as those meant for six soldiers, even though these were for just one officer. She gave a vague nod to another ashigaru who ran past her towards the fences while trying to throw on his armor; no doubt he was a poor soul who'd slept through the change of the guards and had just been scolded by his sergeant.

The officers' tents were all guarded, and beyond the regular soldiers, Atsuko wondered whether there were shinobi waiting in the shadows to intercept any enemy attackers. As for attacking the Emperor himself, that was even more impossible. Takeko had told her that his protection consisted of almost divine warriors, individuals so talented in combat that they could detect the slightest threat in the shadows, men trained from birth to spill their blood in service of the sovereign. Atsuko would have no chance at all and would be spotted within two steps.

But the Emperor wasn't her target, nor were the generals. She veered off before reaching the luxurious tents, still far enough away to avoid being spotted by their bodyguards.

No, what she was interested in was much more practical.

It wasn't long before she found the quartermaster's tent exactly where the sentinel said it would be, in the vicinity of the officers' tents but far enough away to confirm his status as a commoner.

The officers aren't the only ones who know the plans. They're the most obvious targets, the most tempting—but also the best protected. The quartermaster must prepare the horses, organize the supplies, and make sure everyone is ready for their journey. That means he also must know the plans in order to work as efficiently as possible. And no one's going to guard the tent of a simple quartermaster.

Takeko's words floated through Atsuko's mind as she approached her real target.

"Hey—you there, what are you doing here?"

The voice broke the silence of the night, purposefully low so as not to wake everyone, but still charged with authority. Atsuko froze in place, paralyzed with fear.

The sergeant blocking her way barely reached her shoulder. His small stature in an army that put appearance before all else made him more aggressive than necessary, and being assigned to the night shift clearly had done nothing for his mood.

Luckily, her months in the army had prepared the young woman for such a situation. She was too close to the officers' tents to pretend she was on a mission, but there was one plausible excuse:

"I really need to shit, Sergeant," she moaned in her most masculine voice. "Yesterday's rations are wreaking havoc on my stomach."

The officer looked her up and down, and then shrugged his shoulders.

"Yeah, you're not the only one. But that's no reason for you to be skulking about over here. The toilets are at the other end of the camp. What are you hiding?"

Always confess to a lesser crime than what you're actually doing. No one will think you're lying when you admit to something. That's the key to all infiltrations.

"The soldiers' toilets are disgusting," protested Atsuko, holding her nose. "So, I was thinking that maybe the officers' ones—"

The sergeant drew himself up, now sure of his own importance.

"What? You wanted to put your dirty ashigaru ass onto the nobles' shitters? Your poor nose is fragile, is that it? You think you're better than everyone else? Do you know I could have you executed for that?"

"Oh, please, Sergeant, it's not so bad. Can't you turn a blind eye? Just this once?"

Atsuko delicately twirled a few coins she'd taken from the purse of the poor sentinel. If the sergeant wasn't corruptible, she'd have to run, and fast. She'd be lucky to get out alive.

But few sergeants were incorruptible; not with the wages they were currently getting.

The coins disappeared into the sergeant's pocket, who then poked her in the shoulder.

"Go on, get out of here, and don't let me catch you again!"

"So, can I use the officers' toilets, then?"

"You've got to be kidding! Count your lucky stars I'm not reporting you! Get out of here before I change my mind!"

Atsuko didn't push and ran away as fast as she could. It wasn't until the sergeant was far behind her that she slowed down and returned to her mission, taking great care not to bump into him again; the same excuse wouldn't work a second time.

This time, she arrived in front of the quartermaster's tent without interruption. She looked behind her, checked that no one could see her, and then sliced an opening in the fabric with two quick cuts of the tantō. She darted through and readjusted the fabric behind her—the blade was so precise that anyone passing outside wouldn't see the tear unless they came close with a lantern.

If he sleeps with other people—maybe a stable boy or an assistant—you must get rid of them before you wake up your target. Gag them to stop them from crying out and slit their throats, making sure you sever their vocal cords.

Atsuko had come this far without having to spill any blood, and she was comforted to find that the quartermaster slept alone. He wasn't quite important enough to mingle with the nobles but still enough to have his own tent instead of sharing with other soldiers.

She snuck up to his bed and put her hand to his mouth while pressing her knife to his throat. He awoke with a start, his eyes wide, and he desperately attempted to get free. He was strong, but so was Atsuko, and she had a much better position. The sting of the knife at his throat quickly put him in a more cooperative mood.

"I'm going to remove my hand," said Atsuko, feeling like she was repeating herself tonight. "Make a sound and you're dead, understand?"

The quartermaster vigorously nodded his head, and she freed his mouth.

"What do you want?" he asked.

It was all so predictable, in the end. Everyone reacted in the same way, said pretty much the same words, and had a throat that dried up at the cold touch of a blade.

"The plan of attack. Give it to me, and you'll live."

The quartermaster shook his head.

"I can't."

"Then you'll die."

"You'll kill me anyway once I've told you."

They all get there, at one moment or another: negotiation. Nobody wants to die—that's human nature. Give them a path to survival, and they'll take it without hesitation.

"No, I won't kill you," replied Atsuko softly. "If you obey me, I won't touch a hair on your head."

"You're lying," scoffed the quartermaster. "What use would

the information I give you be if you leave me alive? The officers will change the plans the next day, and whatever I told you would be useless."

The teenager smiled, but it was not a reassuring one. It was the smug smile of a cat preparing to toy with a mouse, or of a shark that smelt blood in Osaka Bay. The man readjusted his position in bed and drew the covers up around himself, as if they could protect him from a tantō.

"If you don't talk, you'll definitely die," explained Atsuko calmly. "If you give me the plans, however, I'll leave here, safe in the knowledge you won't breathe a word of this to your superiors."

"And how will you be so sure?" protested the quartermaster. "I can give you my word, but I'm sure that's not enough."

The key to a successful infiltration begins long before the night in question. The more you research your target, the more you can anticipate any problems, and the more tricks you have up your sleeve. Some missions require months of preparatory work. That's part of the job.

"You're right," said Atsuko. "But we know you have a wife and two children—including, of course, the beautiful Chiaki, who's just given birth to a wonderful and perfectly healthy baby boy, as lively and brave as his grandfather. What's his name again? Ah yes, *Seiya*."

"If you dare go near my family—" breathed the man.

He tried to get up, but Atsuko's hand forced him back down.

"Come now, we're not so cruel—on the condition that you hold your tongue, of course. If you refuse to give me the plan of attack, if you try to lie, or if you tell anyone about our little chat, our organization will not hesitate to react appropriately."

"What organization?"

"That's none of your concern. All that matters is that your wife, children, and grandson will live."

The teenager removed her tantō. She no longer needed it; the man was broken. She felt a ball of unease in her stomach and tried to remind herself that she was doing this for her side, for justice, that the Emperor had been manipulated by the other clans, and that they were going to liberate him.

Defeated, the man gave her the plans, and she took a moment to study them before rising from the bed. She stupidly thanked him, as though it had been a chat between friends. The quartermaster only shrugged his shoulders.

"Now, get out of my tent. I won't be held responsible if you're captured."

"But that's exactly what my organization will think," countered Atsuko. "It makes no difference to them whether it was a case of bad luck or a betrayal. All they'll see is that I didn't make it back. And your family—"

"You're lying!"

"Do you really want to take that chance?"

This time the quartermaster really hesitated, but he'd already said too much. Once you'd started on the path, it was easier to keep going than to turn back.

"Fine," he said. "What must I do?"

"Nothing complicated. Just give me a plausible reason to leave camp at this hour. Maybe to look after the horses, or—"

"No," the man cut her off, thinking hard. "The horses are all inside. There's really no valid reason for you to leave camp this late at night. What I can do, however, is allow you to get as far as the barricade. Once you're there, I imagine you won't find it too difficult to disappear. You made it to my bed, so you must have more in your bag of tricks."

Atsuko nodded her head, not letting him see any of her doubts; all the better if he mistook her for a shinobi with exceptional talent. There was less dishonor in conceding to a ninja than a teenager barely older than sixteen.

Imbued with a new sense of purpose now that he'd made the decision, the quartermaster rose from his bed, and this time Atsuko let him. He picked up a piece of parchment from the pile at the foot of his bed and quickly scribbled a requisition order.

"Here. If anyone stops you, tell them the quartermaster ordered two extra blankets for the officers. No one should doubt your word, not with this document. And now," he continued with a grimace, "if you were lying and you plan to kill me anyway, do it now. As painlessly as possible, I beg you."

He put his head back and exposed his throat, and Atsuko took a step back. He really expected her to strike, here and now.

"Come now," she reassured him softly. "What good would your information be if your officers were to find your corpse in the morning? They'd wonder if you'd talked and would alter their plans, just in case. You see, I have my own reasons for not killing you. It's merely a last resort for if you betray me."

He collapsed onto the bed, his relief palpable. Atsuko noticed a urine stain on his trousers, and it suddenly reminded her of her brother; she almost lost her composure and forced herself back into the role she was playing.

"I'm leaving now. I'm counting on you to uphold your part of the deal, and nothing will happen to your family."

"How can I be sure?" asked the man.

We never take a life for pleasure. We won't hesitate to kill when it serves our aims, but we're not cruel.

"We never take a life for pleasure," recited Atsuko as she headed out of the tent. "We won't hesitate to kill when it serves our aims, but we're not cruel."

The quartermaster didn't respond. His eyes were closed in a foolish hope. Was he really going to survive this night?

He heard the movement of fabric as a hand pushed open the flaps of his tent. When he opened his eyes, the stranger had disappeared.

19

Atsuko had started the infiltration with a heavy fear in her heart.

The sentinel could have spotted her before she attacked from behind; they could have refused to surrender and tried to sound the alarm; they might not have known where the quartermaster's tent was; the relief could have arrived earlier than expected; a sergeant might have seen through her disguise; the quartermaster might not have been in his tent; he might have been better guarded than Takeko had thought; and he could have refused to surrender to her threats.

So many things could have gone wrong—but now, Atsuko could breathe easy: the most difficult part was over. She possessed the information she'd come to find, and she even had a prepared excuse in case anyone asked awkward questions. In short, everything had gone well, and she indulged in a satisfied smile.

Maybe she would have actually made it out of the camp with no issues if she hadn't let her guard down too soon.

"Hey, you, what are you doing?"

She turned with a fake smile on her lips and rifled in her pocket to find the letter from the quartermaster.

"They asked me to go and find more blankets for the officers," she explained. "So of course, it had to be me."

She'd done it all perfectly: the deep voice, the learned nonchalance, the little hint of worry every soldier had when being questioned by a superior, even if he was in the right. Yes, everything was perfect, except the way the oversized breastplate had slipped down her shoulder, pulling down the top of her tunic. The sergeant squinted in the half-darkness and held up his lantern to get a better look.

"By all the onis, you—you're a woman? What the hell is a woman doing in our camp?"

Before Atsuko even felt a sense of fear, her first emotion was frustration. Any man would have been able to get out with no issues using the excuse she'd shared. The sub-officers couldn't know every ashigaru in the army and one face among thousands would always pass unnoticed. But a woman? Now, *that* was something that shouldn't be here and unavoidably attracted attention. Yet again, her gender betrayed her.

Of course, Takeko had prepared an excuse for such a scenario. Takeko anticipated absolutely everything.

If your womanhood poses a problem, use it as a weapon. Make them believe you spent the night in a daimyo's tent and that you're heading home. Most of the lower ranks would never dare disturb a master to verify your story, especially at the risk of a scandal. Their career would be over. They'd probably give you the benefit of the doubt.

But Atsuko's mind went blank. She'd relaxed so much at the last minute that her body was just screaming out for rest, and the necessary response wouldn't come to her fast enough. By the time she remembered what she was supposed to say, the moment had passed, and the sergeant grew too suspicious.

"Now, you're going to follow me, sweetie, and no funny business—unless you want me to gut you like a pig."

It was too late for talk. All that remained was violence. She raised her empty hands to show she wasn't armed and gave him her most innocent smile—then hit him in the throat with her outstretched hands.

We don't have the time to turn you into a martial arts expert. You learned the basics in the family dojo but your training was mostly focused on weapons. So just remember this move. A smack to the throat, quick and precise. It doesn't work in a real fight, but if your opponent isn't expecting you to strike, they'll be taken by surprise. The blow can kill, but if not, they'll be too busy trying to breathe to sound the alarm.

That was the theory anyway—and she'd been better at it when she practiced with Takeko. But in the field, half-blinded by the lantern shining in her face and too panicked, she missed her target by a finger's width. The sergeant had time to turn his head and the hand that should have cut off his breath only bounced off his shoulder.

"At arms!" screamed the man, now convinced he was dealing with an enemy. "Intruders in the camp!"

He mustn't have felt confident enough to ring the alarm bell for one person. Nonetheless, his shouts had the desired effect. Warriors stumbled out of their tents, some still half naked, others buckling their belts, and others rubbing sleep out of their eyes.

When the alarm is sounded, there's only one thing left to do: flee. And if you can't manage that, then die with honor.

Atsuko had no desire to die, even if it was with honor. Not after having come so far in her mission. She used the sergeant's distraction to her advantage as he continued to shout, and feinted to the left, then when he tried to block her way, she dodged right. He stumbled and let out a scream of rage, but she was already long gone.

She knocked over a soldier who was still trying to figure out what was going on, feinted around the chest of a more alert warrior who tried to impale her with his lance, then rolled into the opening of a tent to avoid another who tried to grab her by the shoulders. She emerged from the other side, and with a swipe of her tantō cut down the hangings to block the path of her hunters.

Atsuko had no chance of escaping a full camp, but she refused to give up. All that mattered was reaching the palisade, just a few yards away. A man much larger than the others stood in front of her, and without stopping, without hesitation, without even thinking, she grabbed his testicles in an iron grip. He wailed as she twisted, the light of defiance leaving his eyes. She continued her run, shaking her hand as if she could wash away the atrocious contact.

The only thing that saved her was the chaos in the camp. Nobody knew what was going on, and some were preparing for an all-out attack while others worried that the food stocks had been stolen. Soldiers ran in all directions, while officers shouted contradictory orders and tried with no success to restore order. The Imperial forces lit lamps to see better, then rubbed their eyes, unable to adjust to such bright light. Atsuko saw two warriors fighting on the ground, each convinced the other was an intruder.

"They're over here!" shouted someone.

"They're coming from the West!" screamed another.

A dry explosion reverberated, acting as a painful reminder to Atsuko that the Imperial camp had more firearms than the Shogun camp. If she was caught in the sights of a gunner, not even her dexterity could save her.

On instinct, she ducked, running hunched over like Takeko had taught her. A katana almost decapitated her, but she ducked further, rolled onto her shoulder, and kept running without any wasted movement. The samurai lost a few seconds while following her with his eyes incredulously before finally setting off in pursuit.

She eventually arrived at the palisade as chaos continued to reign in the camp. Three sentinels turned towards her with the lances readied for action, and she once again disguised her voice.

"They're coming! Quick! Close the gates! The Shogun army is trying to escape!"

"Huh? Escape?" stammered one of the warriors.

Instinctively, two of them turned to watch the town as though soldiers would be running from buildings. The third was less trusting and squinted his eyes to get a better look at her.

"Which unit do you belong to? Who did this order come from?"

His mistrust was admirable, but it did him no good. Without slowing her run, Atsuko thrust her hand forwards and a metallic shine flew towards the warrior. He felt a strike against his chest and lowered his eyes to see a tantō deeply embedded into his heart.

"Oh," he said, as she passed him and leapt to grab onto the palisade.

He was already dead by the time she climbed on top of the palisade and slid over the top. In the meantime, his two comrades had finally realized what was happening; one of them grabbed a bow and arrow while the other's shouts blended into the confusion of the camp:

"Intruder! Intruder!"

Atsuko rolled to the ground and set off, running in a zigzag towards the town. She felt more than saw an arrow strike near her feet, then a second got lost in the vegetation. Spurred on by survival instinct, she found a way to accelerate even more.

She risked a glance behind her and grimaced upon seeing that some soldiers had continued to pursue her despite the confusion. Four silhouettes ran after her, and the gates opened to let pass three samurai on horseback.

Now, that was the most worrying thing. While Atsuko was willing to bet that she could lose her pursuers on foot, the horses complicated things. If she didn't reach the town before they reached her, all was lost.

Her heart almost beat out of her chest, blood rushed to her temples, her legs burned, and she could feel the beginning of a stitch in her side. She wasn't worried about the first three sensations because she knew her own limits and knew she could continue, but the last symptom was concerning. If the pain increased, she wouldn't be able to keep moving so quickly.

That's just a myth; clenching your fist is absolutely no help when you get a stitch—but it makes you feel like you're doing something to fight the pain, and that's just as important.

Myth or not, and because she lacked any better solution, she clenched her fists as tightly as she could.

Behind her, the horses were gaining ground, and Atsuko realized that she wouldn't make it to the forest in time. Her hand reached for her tantō before she remembered that she'd abandoned it in the sentinel's heart. That was so stupid of her! Now she had no way of defending herself at all.

In despair for her lost cause, Atsuko threw the last of her strength into sprinting, but she could already feel the horses' hooves as they shook the ground just behind her. There was just one card left to play—if it didn't work, she was dead.

Noble steeds are used to battlefields from a young age, and not much can surprise them. They're loyal animals who obey their masters from the slightest touch, even in the midst of carnage. Only not all horses are noble steeds. Most of the scouts and even low-ranking samurai have much more classic horses who haven't been through the same training and can be more nervous.

Atsuko counted the rhythm of the horses' hooves: one, two, three, four, then she spun to face them and rose to her full height, both arms outstretched.

"*AAAAAAAAAAAH!*" she screamed with everything left in her lungs.

The samurai had been perched on the edge of his saddle, ready to strike out with his katana, and he wasn't holding on to the reins—so there was nothing he could do when his horse reared upwards. He fell to the ground with a clattering of armor and rolled into a ball to prevent his skull from being trampled by hooves. Just behind him, the two other horses had to change direction so as not to run him over.

Atsuko again set off at a run with her heart in her mouth, but this time it was all over. Her stitch was making her suffer and she was losing breath, and she had no more tricks up her sleeve.

She was very surprised to reach the town walls a few seconds before the horses. She took the first street on the left, shimmied down two alleys, jumped up to grab the sign of an ironmonger, swung herself onto the roof and hid like a child. She knew these streets like the back of her hand. No one could find her here!

Behind her, the samurai pulled on the reins and came to a complete stop. Horses were costly and no one was stupid enough to gallop into a town with narrow streets in the middle of the night. That was a sure way for a horse to break a leg and end up in the abattoir.

Atsuko's respite was short-lived. The pursuers on foot weren't far behind and they wouldn't hesitate to search the streets. Other silhouettes continued to emerge from the camp; soon, she'd be in the midst of a full-scale hunt.

She'd hoped to be able to rest, but she had no choice but to keep running. Atsuko heard a shout behind her as she jumped across to the nearest roof, though she was still far ahead. She ran with everything she could muster to increase the distance between them and leapt almost twelve feet to reach the wall across the alley. She let herself slide down to the ground and took a path that would look like an impasse to her hunters—but that ended in a tree she'd climbed many times. She grabbed onto the lowest branch, hoisted herself up and carried on her escape, now certain she'd outrun them all.

Atsuko continued until she reached the moat and found the bag she'd abandoned earlier in the bushes. All she had to do was swim a few yards, find her rope, and her mission would be a total success.

She took in a huge gasp of air, then another, and they had the most delicious taste. She had accomplished her mission and she was still alive. She began laughing like a crazy person, though the laughs sounded like sobs that soon turned into tears. She didn't know if she was happy, exhausted, or sad; every emotion tumbled out of her, and it was almost too much.

And then the cold blade of a katana appeared out of nowhere to rest at her throat, and she froze on a final inhale.

"Now, now, why these tears? If I'd managed to escape an entire camp of enemies alone, I'd be ecstatic."

Atsuko recognized the voice before she even raised her eyes. He hadn't changed a bit: he still had the same amused smile, the same badly cut hair—and the same skill with a katana.

"It's you," she gasped. "You're the one who attacked daimyo Kayano!"

"And you're the one who stopped me," confirmed Masajiro. "The reports weren't very clear, but a sergeant told me about a woman disguised as a man, and I immediately thought of you."

"How did you manage to catch up to me?" she asked. "I should have been long gone by the time it took you to find that trail."

"That's true," admitted the samurai without a crack in his smile, "but you didn't have many options in your escape, right? My brutes of comrades are all looking for you in town. Meanwhile, it wasn't too difficult for me to realize you'd return to the castle to make your report. All I had to do was wait for you on the banks of the moat and look for traces of footprints."

"Traces of…?"

"The snow has melted, but you can still see a few footprints," explained Masajiro benevolently. "Would you believe, I'm just as good a tracker as I am a swordsman."

Atsuko couldn't help but laugh at his raised eyebrow, as though he wasn't an enemy, or she wasn't at his mercy, or he couldn't decapitate her with one small slice of his sword.

The enormity of her situation hit her. She had already fought against Masajiro; even with a katana she'd barely managed to hold onto her head. Without any weapons, this was suicide.

"It looks like I'm your prisoner," she admitted, the taste of defeat like bile in her throat.

"It looks like," he agreed.

Masajiro looked around them and then, in a swift movement, removed his katana. He offered his hand to help her stand, and—too stunned to expect a trap—she accepted it.

"But on the other hand, you left me alive the last time you could have killed me. So I think the least I could do in return is to let you go."

Atsuko stared at him incredulously, unable to believe her luck.

"I'm free? Really?"

"At least until we meet again. Now we're even. Next time, we'll be enemies again. It's a shame. I would have preferred us to be on the same side. There are so few women as beautiful, brave, ingenious, or skilled in combat on the Imperial side. Are there many in the Shogun's camp?"

"So many," affirmed Atsuko, crossing her arms. "You'll see on the battlefield."

"Ah, I knew I chose the wrong side," chuckled the samurai as he turned to leave. "But what's done is done. That being said, I can't keep calling you *young woman*. It's disrespectful. Can I know your name?"

She could have answered with anything. But it was the truth that came to her lips.

"Atsuko."

"Nice to meet you, Atsuko. My name is Masajiro."

He gave an exaggerated bow and turned to observe the town. They could both hear calls and shouts in the distance.

"They'll be here soon. If I were you, I wouldn't dawdle. Go home to your people, Atsuko-of-Shogun."

"Enjoy your night, Masajiro-of-Emperor."

"Oh, I sleep like a baby, except for when women with short hair get it in their heads to wake up an entire camp."

With these parting words, the samurai pivoted on his heel and returned to the town. Atsuko watched him go for a few seconds, a light smile on her face.

Beautiful, brave, ingenious, and skilled in combat.

He was talking about her.

20

Matsudaira Katamori looked at the plans in his hand, his expression indecipherable.

"You say these are authentic?"

"Yes, Master," confirmed Takeko, bowing as low as she could.

"It's all in here: the weaknesses they think they've found in the walls, the times they want to launch a fake attack to tire our defenses, the time of the real offensive. There's even the number of cannons they have, and the time they think it will take to cause a breach! It's a miracle! With such information, we could actually win this war—or at the very least, this battle."

He dropped the plans onto his desk, more enthusiastic than he'd been in months, since the beginning of this string of defeats at the hands of the Emperor. For the first time, they could have the advantage.

"The full shogunate—or at least what's left of it—owes you a great debt, Lady Takeko. If there's anything I can do for you, please don't hesitate to ask and I will do my utmost to satisfy the request."

The spy bowed low once more.

"My only hope is to serve your cause to the best of my abilities, Master. And I have a proposition for you. You are aware that the army refuses to accept women into its ranks. However, many girls, women, wives, and widows wish to fight for their freedom. You need every possible troop to survive against the Emperor. Don't refuse their help."

"Do you have any idea how that would make us look?" protested the daimyo with a frown. "We'd be the laughingstock of all the regions!"

"What's more important, Master? That you win the battle, or that you uphold outdated principles? Once upon a time, women fought at the sides of men, and no one batted an eye."

"Yes the *omna-bugeisha*," replied Katamori. "I've heard some call you that. But you're exceptional, Takeko. Other women aren't like you. I don't need weepers in my army."

The spy clenched her fists but maintained her calm. The most important changes always started with a small victory, which felt like nothing in the moment.

"You underestimate these 'weepers,'" she stated with pursed lips. "For example, who do you think succeeded in stealing these plans right from under the nose of the enemy?"

"A woman? Really?" stammered the daimyo.

"A teenage girl," corrected Takeko with a sweet smile. "Atsuko, won't you come and join us?"

She had raised her voice on these final words and in response, someone knocked on the door.

"May she come in?" asked the spy.

"That's your miracle teenager?" muttered Katamori. "Well, I… yes, go ahead, let her in."

Takeko opened the door and Atsuko stepped into the room, her eyes to the floor. Just a year ago, she'd been presented to the daimyo to see if any of his men wanted to marry her. How things changed.

"So, you're the one who infiltrated the Imperial camp?" asked the daimyo.

"Yes, Master."

The man turned towards Takeko, still doubtful.

"Fine, I believe that she could pass unnoticed. But to fight? War is man's business."

"Give Atsuko a yari and let her fight any one of your men. I know who I'd bet on."

"You can't be serious!" Katamori burst out laughing, before frowning. "Oh, you are serious."

"Of course, if she wins, it would be quite embarrassing," admitted Takeko.

The daimyo studied the young women in front of him again and then dropped into his seat, depressed.

"How far will we degrade ourselves? Fine, very well. What do you want?"

"Simply the authorization for women who want to join my unit. Officially, they won't be a part of the army, which will resolve your moral quandary. But we would be available to defend the castle walls."

"I did promise you a reward, huh?" said Katamori. "Don't let it be said that I don't keep my word. Very well, Takeko. Form your unit. Anyway, it's not like you'll be able to enjoy it for long. One way or another, the end is near."

Atsuko hadn't seen her brother in almost six months. They had briefly crossed paths after the battle and Atsuko had wanted to tell him what she'd done for him, but his first words were:

"You were wrong, little sister! You thought I'd flee, but I was covered in glory! I was one of the only survivors of our unit and the daimyo has given me a new distinction!"

"I'm happy for you," breathed Atsuko.

Lies! Nothing but lies! She could have forgiven him if he'd accepted the situation, if he'd admitted that he'd fled yet again. And she would have told him that it was okay, that she loved him all the same, that they'd always be brother and sister, and that she'd even killed for him.

But this lie, after the betrayal in the village, had put an end to their relationship. She hadn't tried to renew any contact.

So it was a surprise when she saw him walk into the room she now shared with Takeko on the second floor of the castle.

"Am I disturbing you?" he asked, hesitantly.

"That's never stopped you before," she replied, with more venom than she would have liked.

He shrugged his shoulders and sat down next to her on the bed.

"The final battle approaches, and this time I definitely won't be able to flee as usual. It's difficult to flee when the enemies are encircling us, right?"

"I thought you'd found your courage during our last battle?"

"I lied to you," he admitted, lowering his eyes. "I was—I was afraid you'd judge me. During that battle, I completely lost control of my nerves and I—I fled to the forest. I even climbed a tree so no one would spot me. I stayed there for three hours, chilled to the bone and wondering if the fight was over. And then I came down and slipped in amongst a few survivors and returned to camp. Everyone welcomed me as a hero. Can you imagine? I was the only survivor in a unit of a hundred samurai! They were all convinced I'd survived because I fought like a demon. Not a single one thought I'd ran away."

The silence hung heavily between them, and Ibuka finally looked up at her.

"You hate me, don't you?"

"A little," admitted Atsuko. "But no more than before. I knew, you know. I watched you flee. And your lies these last few months really hurt me."

He opened his mouth, closed it, and opened it again, for the first time completely lost for words. Then he laughed out loud, a laugh that had always been his trademark.

"I should have known. It's always a mistake to try and hide things from you. Anyway, here we are, and I had hoped you could forgive me, and we could reconcile."

The two stared into each other's eyes and Atsuko suddenly understood. For the first time, Ibuka was at peace. He was convinced he was going to die, and this certainty had transcended his fear. He wanted to win his sister's forgiveness before he moved on.

"I heard Takeko is building an entirely female unit," began her brother. "I suppose you'll be a part of it?"

"Possibly," admitted Atsuko. "Why?"

"The samurai will definitely be executed or held for ransom. But most of the women, and especially those from good blood, will be spared. If you didn't fight, maybe—"

"No."

"Maybe you'd be spared—"

"No."

"All I'm saying is—"

"No."

"I don't want you to die or be injured. You already saved my life. Now let me save yours."

"By telling me to hide with the children and those incapable of fighting? I've told you three times already, but I will repeat: *No*. I'm more skilled that most of your comrades. Takeko's unit will make the difference. And I'll be with them."

Atsuko shielded her eyes to better see the army massing in front of them. She hadn't taken the time to read the plans she'd stolen in much detail, and she didn't know where they were eventually going to attack, though that wasn't important. There were so many of them! And they were so well armed!

She saw men rolling cannons along the sodden ground, while the machine gun operators waited patiently to be called to action. The soldiers checked their guns and ensured the gunpowder hadn't gotten wet.

Meanwhile, Aizu's defenders were climbing onto the ramparts armed with bows and arrows.

For the first time, seeing the imbalance in the armies, Atsuko felt that she would not survive. She had always fought to become a samurai, but she'd been born in the wrong time. The samurai would soon be consigned to history, relegated to the footnotes of heavy manuals on firearms and military discipline.

Atsuko studied her surroundings to take comfort in the unit she'd been incorporated into. An exclusively female corps composed of fifteen women—among them, the sister and mother of Takeko. Brave women who'd taken up arms to defend their castle, even though they'd never fought before today.

Atsuko couldn't help but compare them to her brother: he was so talented but wasted it all. These women weren't at all gifted, but they were ready to give their lives.

Takeko sensed her troubles, and gently squeezed her hand.

"Everything will be alright," she whispered. "Even if we fall, no one will forget us. We are breathing history. We are a female army. We are the *Joshitai*."

21

A pale sun rose to illuminate the castle. Just as the plans acquired by Atsuko had suggested, the enemy assembled around the moat, ready to launch multiple attacks to distract the defenders before concentrating all its forces on the western ramparts.

It was one thing to anticipate such a move, but it was another thing entirely to counter it. Matsudaira Katamori had amassed his best soldiers there to delay the inevitable breach, but he had concocted an even more audacious strategy himself. He had brought together all the horses he could find along with his best samurai. They all faced the portcullis, ready to attempt a breakthrough upon which the result of this battle depended.

"It's no use defending ourselves against such force," began the daimyo. "Even if we push back this attack, there will be another, and then another, until we can no longer protect our ramparts. The true danger comes from the cannons that threaten our walls. If we can manage to destroy their artillery, we have a chance. We know where they're going to fire, and when. We're going to take a little outing, destroy their cannons, and return to the safety of the castle before they even know what happened."

The katana he'd retrieved after Kayano's murder shone brightly in his hand, the famous katana for which Lloyd had fought so hard, and the heritage of Musashi.

"Freedom or death!" he cried. "For the Shogun!"

"Freedom or death!" shouted the soldiers in unison.

None of them mentioned Tokugawa. To them, he was the traitor who'd gotten them into this mess.

A horse approached at trot, with a feminine silhouette astride, and Katamori let out an irritated groan.

"What now, Lady Takeko? You have your unit of women, so what more do you want?"

"To fight, that's what I want," replied the young woman. "We're ready to fight to the death. Your breakthrough must succeed if we're to stand the slightest chance of survival. We're coming with you."

"Absolutely not," grumbled the daimyo. "Your enthusiasm is admirable, but I need trustworthy soldiers who I know and who I've already done battle with."

He lowered his voice before adding:

"I'm not doubting your competence. But understand, the mission I gave you is just as important!"

"Defending the ramparts?" snorted Takeko. "Anyone could do that. We'd be more useful in the middle of enemy forces."

All goodwill disappeared from the daimyo's face.

"I've been very patient with you. Now let me rephrase this so you understand: that is an order. An order, you understand? Your unit will be good girls and stay on the outer walls and stop anyone who tries to set foot there. Is that clear?"

"Very clear," grumbled the young woman before turning her horse around.

The daimyo watched her leave before rolling his eyes.

"Ah, women!" he whined to the laughter of his comrades. "Right. Prepare to charge!"

Lloyd checked on the sharpness of his katana and broke into a cruel smile as a drop of blood appeared on his finger.

"I wish you'd stop doing that," observed Harry Parkes, dabbing his lips with a handkerchief. "You know I don't like the sight of blood."

"I saw you shoot a bullet right into a spy's forehead."

"Maybe so, but I closed my eyes while they cleaned it up," protested the consul. "Heavens above, William, don't be such a caricature every time. If you must verify that your sword can cut, use a sheet of parchment or another method to your liking."

Instead of replying, Lloyd opened the flaps of his tent to observe the soldiers. Just one more battle and the Boshin war would be no more than a sad memory. Just one more battle and the Emperor's throne would be definitively secured, away from the influence of the Shogun and the daimyos. Japan was about to enter the modern age—guided by the British, of course.

And the Templars, obviously.

"Isn't Mutsuhito expecting you in the capital, anyway?"

"Ah! So you want to get rid of me?"

"Let's just say your place isn't really on the battlefield."

The consul set down the cup of tea he was sipping and put on his gloves with deliberate slowness.

"Rest assured, I just wanted to check that the situation was under control. Her Majesty the Queen is curious to see how our Japanese friends come out of this. They must win this battle, Lloyd. Our commercial treaties depend on it."

The Templar calmly sheathed his weapon.

"They'll win it."

Wind whistled through the barbicans as the Imperial forces gave the order to attack. The morning's calm was broken by the sudden rumbling of the cannons. The walls of the castle shook and ladders were slammed up against them. Soon there were hundreds of soldiers climbing up them, eager to be the first to set foot on the ramparts.

"Now's the time!" shouted Katamori. "Open the gates!"

With a heavy rumbling, the drawbridge lowered to the great surprise of the attackers. They had expected a series of desperate moves, but a direct charge hadn't featured among them. The gunners prepared to turn the cannons while the reserve soldiers attempted to face down the threat.

It was no use. The Imperial soldiers, made overconfident by their consistent victories and technological superiority, had no chance in melee against the fine flower of Aizu, the last samurai in Japan. They fell in droves as the cannons stopped firing, one by one.

Chaos reigned on the ramparts, as the Imperial soldiers were left wondering whether they should climb back down, while orders were not incoming.

"Oh, by all the hells of Dante," grumbled Lloyd. "Do I have to do everything myself around here?"

He emerged from his tent like a fury, jumped onto the back of a horse and spurred it on in the direction of the battle. He decapitated an enemy from behind before running another through, using the movement for balance.

"No retreat! We've got them cornered! Reinforcements are on the way!"

He wasn't the only one to note the huge number of enemies they were up against. The generals were regaining their confidence and ordering units of gunners back into position.

Lloyd gave a smirk of satisfaction when he saw a glimmering on his right side. He twisted in his saddle and released himself from the stirrups as a blade of dazzling beauty passed within a hair's breadth of his head.

"Coward!" growled Matsudaira Katamori. "Fight me!"

In one glance, Lloyd recognized the blade he'd been searching for this entire time, the weapon that would be his redemption among the Order of the Templars, the symbol that would solidify the power of the Emperor—along with his own.

"Oh, with pleasure," he grinned, raising his own sword.

No one had set foot on the ramparts yet, and Takeko watched the combat below with a growing frustration.

"I won't stay here twiddling my thumbs while the daimyo fights for freedom," she growled. "If he falls, everything is lost anyway."

"But he ordered us to stay here," protested Atsuko. "If we disobey..."

"Ha!" said the spy. "What do you think he'll do to us, exactly? If we lose the battle, we die anyway. And if we win, well, given the probabilities, I'm ready to accept any punishment he wants to give me."

Put like that, it was an easy decision to make. The fifteen women looked at each other and solemnly nodded their heads. Some knew how to fight and some had only recently learned, but they all burned with righteous fire. Takeko had found them spare naginatas from the army; only Atsuko kept her trusty lance.

"By the time we get there, the battle will be over," protested a woman old enough to be a grandmother—in all likelihood, she probably was one.

"There's a shortcut! Follow me!"

A shortcut? Intrigued, Atsuko watched her mentor as she sprinted down the stairs and burst into a room on the first floor. With no hesitation, Takeko leapt out of the window and landed in the moat below.

"That's her shortcut?" stuttered the old woman.

"She's completely crazy!" confirmed another warrior.

"No, she's right," countered Atsuko. "A fall from this height shouldn't be painful, and the cold will be the least of our worries in battle. It's not as though we're wearing breastplates anyway."

"But..."

Without waiting for the others to respond, the teenager also jumped out of the window, and for the second time in days, she found herself up to her neck in icy moat water. She kicked her legs weakly and reached the banks where Takeko was already waiting. By jumping, she had just bought them precious seconds, or even minutes. In a battle like this, time was crucial… so long as the rest of the Joshitai followed them.

Several splashes assured her that they had. Every single one of the warriors surfaced, spitting and coughing. Some of their teeth were chattering, but that didn't make them any less determined.

"Female company, charge!" cried Takeko.

She charged at the backs of the Imperials circling the daimyo. The soldiers weren't at all expecting an attack from this side, and her naginata sliced through them like wheat. The ones who finally turned around to face the attacker were subsequently met with Atsuko's blows and then fell.

But the element of surprise could only last so long, and the pressure soon built on the Joshitai. Out of the corner of her eye, Atsuko saw a mother twirl her naginata and impale two enemies in one move, but not all were so skilled. One by one, they fell on the banks, covered in blood.

With a supreme effort, Atsuko finally managed to break through the line of defense to join the daimyo's soldiers. Gasping and bleeding from multiple wounds, Katamori looked them up and down.

"Didn't I tell you to stay inside?"

"Punish us later!" shouted Takeko, rising to her full height.

"I shouldn't say this, but I'm glad to see you," he rasped. "Let's just say I might have overestimated our forces a bit."

"The Joshitai are here to assist you!" rallied Takeko.

Her naginata twirled from left to right, and enemies dropped like flies. Triumphant, Takeko sunk back into the defensive stance.

"So, what were you saying about women?"

A detonation echoed in the distance and a bullet from a gun crossed the battlefield to hit Takeko in the chest. She put her hand to her chest and stared at it, covered in blood. Incredulity hung on her face as her legs slowly folded beneath her.

"Takeko! No!" screamed Atsuko.

It was not possible. Her mentor was invincible. She wasn't afraid of anything, not even death. She'd shown that when she jumped out of the window without missing a beat. How could an anonymous bullet put an end to the life of such an extraordinary woman? Didn't she deserve a long duel with a master swordsman at sunset while the shadows danced around them?

Atsuko knelt next to Takeko to see if she could be saved, but her mentor only gave her a weak and bloody smile.

"I don't want… them to get my head," she managed to croak out. "That they celebrate… that they… killed me… that they parade it… in the capital."

"What?" said Atsuko, between her mentor's dying breaths.

"Cut off my head... and throw it... in the moat..."

"I can't do that! I can't do it!"

"I'm already... dead, Atsuko. It's my last request. I... beg you."

Atsuko rose, nodding her head, but Takeko's eyes had already glossed over. It was the last request of a dying woman.

Through a flurry of tears, and paying no heed to the fight, crying for the only person who'd ever understood her, Atsuko grabbed Takeko's naginata.

Just one swipe, and her head rolled to the ground.

Atsuko picked it up by the hair, took a deep breath, and threw it into the moat. The head spun through the air before disappearing under the water's surface, taking with it the memory of Takeko, the last samurai in Japan.

Atsuko turned around and had no time to dry her eyes before a man jumped in front of her with a bloody katana in his hand. By reflex, she lurched forward to strike his stomach, but he deflected the blow easily.

"I beg you, take me a little more seriously than that, won't you?"

With no response to his sarcasm and narrowed eyes, Atsuko delivered another attack, but once more he blocked her. She attempted to strike his legs and he jumped over her hilt. She tried to slit his throat with her yari and he struck the weapon from her left hand. She wanted to hit him, but he jumped away at the last second and she fell to the ground.

And Atsuko understood, for the first time, just how strong he was.

Stronger than the brigand she'd defeated on the road.

Stronger than the samurai she'd fought to defend Musashi's sword.

Stronger than the handsome Masajiro.

Stronger than Uesegi.

Stronger even than her brother.

Her brother!

In all of this, she hadn't even looked to see if he was still alive. If the Imperials had hurt him… if they had killed him…

She looked behind her as if by a sixth sense, and saw that he too was curled up on the ground. He'd abandoned his horse, or maybe he'd fallen off. He was babbling incoherently, incapable of fighting, overwhelmed by yet another bout of terror.

All this for that.

All that for this.

And that briefest slip in concentration was her undoing as Lloyd's blade traced a wide slit in her stomach. Blood poured out of her, and the pain nearly made her lose consciousness.

Then the hilt of the Englishman's katana hit her squarely in the face, and it was a relief to collapse into unconsciousness.

Death wasn't so scary after all. Why had her brother never

understood that? She would see her father again.

Her mother.

Takeko.

And soon probably Ibuka, too.

22

Atsuko's cries of pain broke through the cloud surrounding Ibuka. How was it possible? His sister was supposed to be on the ramparts, far from the fighting. He'd argued for hours with the daimyo to make his point and convince him to keep the Joshitai as the rear guard.

"They fight like demons and the enemy will be surprised to see female troops," Katamori had insisted. "Plus, I trust Takeko and the other girl, the young one with the short hair."

"But they might distract us. We need cohesion! And protecting the ramparts is just as essential."

That was all Ibuka could do for her. In any case, she never would have wanted his help. No doubt she had been furious to learn she was assigned to the rear guard.

But this way, her life would be saved. If the daimyo fell during this suicide mission, maybe the armies would sign a treaty.

His plan had been perfect.

So why could he hear Atsuko's voice now?

Ibuka opened his eyes and returned to reality. The battle surrounded him with the violence he'd always abhorred. The bodies of the soldiers mixed with the corpses of the horses. The blood colored the grass purple, and the sky itself had a red hue.

Kenshiro, a samurai he'd often joked with, gave him a hateful glare as he clashed swords with two enemies.

"Coward," he managed to spit from the corner of his lips.

Coward.

The word was out. This time, he could no longer escape his reputation. Everyone, every single person, had seen him jump from his horse to curl up on the ground while crying like a baby. He would never recover from such a humiliation.

The only thing that kept him going was the cry he heard.

Atsuko's cry.

He looked desperately around and suddenly saw his sister lying beaten on the ground. Blood was pouring out of a serious wound to her stomach, and she'd die if no one came to her aid. He ran forwards to reach her, but a man stood in front of him. The man wasn't Japanese.

"Demon!" growled the daimyo, suddenly jumping out from behind Ibuka. "England must be ashamed to support our enemies like this."

"Is France ashamed of helping you? Don't be such a sore loser," replied Lloyd, getting into the defensive stance.

Katamori was a decent swordsman, but he's never been one of the greats. His talent was nothing compared to Atsuko, Ibuka, Takeko or any of the hatamoto in his service. He was a capable strategist, a fine politician, and a generous man, but duels were not his specialty.

So was it really a surprise that it only took two blows from Lloyd to decapitate him?

The daimyo's body still sat on his horse as hope died among his defenders. The head rolled to the ground and Musashi's sword dropped into the mud, two steps away from Ibuka.

Automatically, Ibuka seized the katana. He whispered to himself that it was a Masamune, and he raised an eyebrow in wonder at its perfect balance in his hand, as though it had been made for him. But that was impossible, of course.

"That weapon. I've been searching for that weapon for months. It belongs to me. Give it to me!" growled Lloyd as he advanced.

The Englishman lurched and without thinking, Ibuka blocked the blow. It reminded him of something, another fight under different circumstances. Lloyd must have remembered too, because his expression changed.

"The coward swordsman! That's all I needed! I promised I'd kill you the next time we saw each other, and now I have all the time in the world. The situation is reversed; this time the reinforcements are coming from my side, not yours!"

Ibuka was barely listening. His eyes darted down to his sister, searching for a sign she was still breathing. He was relieved to see that she was. Atsuko was pale, but she was still breathing. Even from afar, he could see it.

Lloyd's attack took him by surprise, and he got into the defensive stance purely out of reflex, blocking one attack after another. This sword was incredible! But the British man was a remarkable warrior and he eventually found Ibuka's weak spot. The third attack was faster and more vicious, and Ibuka didn't manage to entirely block it. The blade bit into his upper stomach, an identical wound to his sister's. Only in his case, the steel plunged deeper.

"You've gutted me," he stated in a tone of surprise.

Lloyd lowered his katana and checked the damage with a clinical eye.

"Yes, I don't think you'll survive. The wound is deep. Even if I leave you alone, you'd have what, twenty minutes? Thirty? I'm sorry, my boy, but like I said, I need that sword."

He moved forwards to rip the Masamune from Ibuka's hand, but the sword blocked him and made him step back. Lloyd frowned.

"What, you can't deal with the agony? Do you want me to finish you now? You only have to ask."

He stepped forwards again and Ibuka stopped him with the hilt of the blade.

"It's funny," stammered the young man.

"What's funny?" asked Lloyd, returning to the defensive stance.

"All my life… I've been afraid of death… and now, here it is."

"Probably."

"Whatever I do… I won't… escape it."

"That's likely."

"I can't… run away…"

"Clearly."

"In a… certain way… that's… incredibly… liberating."

Lloyd switched to the offensive, but Ibuka blocked him again before counterattacking for the first time. The British man had to leap back to avoid the blow he had not anticipated.

"This is ridiculous," he growled. "You're on the precipice of death. Stop fighting!"

"On the contrary… I can… finally… fight back… for the first time ever. What… have I got… to be frightened of… now?"

He put his left hand on his wound to compress it and force his organs to stay inside, while he got into the defensive stance with his right hand.

"This is ridiculous!" repeated Lloyd. "You're in no state to contend with me, even if you wanted to. Let's stop this childishness."

"Come on… I only have… one hand…" replied Ibuka with a weak smile. "Don't tell me… you're scared?"

He felt blood bubbling at his lips and knew he didn't have long. A lesser warrior would have simply stepped back and waited for all his blood to spill out. But Lloyd seemed mesmerized by the Masamune, which compelled him to finish the fight quickly before any other Imperial soldiers tried to intervene and steal his prize.

Ibuka didn't need to hold for twenty minutes, or even five. This fight would be decided in a matter of seconds, as always.

You were right, little sister: I was a coward until the end, thought Ibuka with a quick glance at his sister. *Can you ever forgive me?*

Lloyd took advantage of the moment to hurtle forwards with both hands on his katana in an attack from high to low intended to cut this petulant boy in two. But Ibuka had anticipated it and understood the distraction technique. He jumped to the side, faster than humanly possible. The effort further opened his wound and he removed his hand, projecting a spurt of blood directly into Lloyd's eye. The Englishman cried out, stumbling backwards, and he couldn't raise his guard in time to block the next attack.

He kept the same expression of surprise on his face as his head landed in the mud.

Ibuka knelt on the ground, his face resolute.

"Some might say that wasn't very honorable, but I was never honorable anyway, right?"

All around him, the tumult of the battle continued. The Shogun's soldiers were waning in number and the fate of the battle was already decided. Japan's future belonged to the Emperor.

But it wasn't Japan's fate that worried Ibuka.

He shakily crawled over to his sister. She was still alive. He grabbed her by the shoulders, and as though he had any chance, tried to carry her out of the battlefield.

Three soldiers attempted to block his path, but he cut them down quickly without slowing, and the others recoiled with no desire to confront this ghost covered in blood and visibly dying, carrying a girl on his shoulders who was nearly as wounded.

"He'll lose all his blood first," observed one man.

"Ten minutes?"

"I give him fifteen."

"Anyone want to bet?"

Soon, as the battle concluded, gathered soldiers were betting on how long the young man had left to live. Until a samurai interrupted their game.

"What is all this?"

"Nothing at all," babbled a soldier.

"Is this how you treat prisoners of war?"

"Prisoners?" protested a man. "They're not prisoners! Look, the boy is still fighting!"

"And you're betting on his survival? Don't you have anything better to do? Get out of here and back to the fight! I'll take care of these two."

"You can't do that—"

"Does anyone want to challenge me? Would someone like to take it up with the Emperor?"

The soldiers looked at each other in hesitation. They knew the samurai and his fiery temper. They had survived this war so far, and there was no sense in dying in the final remaining minutes.

"Of course not, Masajiro. They're all yours."

Epilogue

When Atsuko regained consciousness, she had no idea where she was. A stream trickled happily in a laughing forest drawn straight from a fairy tale.

There was no trace of the battle, of blood or of any Imperial soldiers. She was alone in the middle of a clearing. Tight bandages wrapped around her torso, the only evidence of the fight that had taken place. Without those, she'd have assumed she was still dreaming.

Atsuko looked around but saw no trace of her yari. She rummaged desperately under her tunic and let out a sigh of relief when her fingers closed over her tantō. At least she wasn't entirely unarmed.

A branch snapped and she turned her head. She tried to move into a better combat position, but the pain was overwhelming and she quickly collapsed again.

"You should rest. I've rarely seen such serious wounds from the battlefield, and I've been doing this for over ten years."

"Ma—Masajiro?"

The samurai stepped out of the woods and gave her a small smile. He carried blankets in his arms and a precariously balanced soup pot.

"Before I come any closer, I want to be sure you won't cut me with your knife. You're the type to do that, and I have to say, I saved your life, so it would be quite rude of you."

Atsuko hesitated for a moment before slowly lowering her tantō. It wasn't as though she trusted the samurai, but she'd seen him in action. Without the element of surprise—which was clearly already ruined—she had no chance of hitting him with such a short blade.

"What happened?"

The samurai wrapped a blanket around her shoulders and then sat down beside her with a more somber expression than usual.

"I'll share a short summary, then I'll give you a minute to process. You've been unconscious for a week. Your side lost. The shogunal forces are in retreat. Emperor Mutsuhito will officially take the throne and change his name. Your daimyo is dead. Your brother, too. He saved your life and fought to the death to protect you. I'm sorry."

Atsuko was listening to the news as though it held no interest for her. What did she care who sat on the throne? She had lost, and that was that. But the mention of her brother caused her to cry out and curl up into a ball on the floor.

"Ibuka… it can't be."

"He died a hero," said Masajiro softly.

"You wouldn't say that if you knew him," sobbed Atsuko. "He was… he was anything but a hero. And he can't be dead!"

"He died a hero," Masajiro repeated, slightly louder. "Whether you believe it or not doesn't change anything."

The teenager cried, sobbed, insisted that the samurai was lying, demanded proof, cried some more, rolled on the ground and reopened her wound, until Masajiro had to forcibly hold her down to re-tie her bandages.

Later—much later—when she'd finally calmed down, she looked over at the man making tea above the fire.

"Did he really die a hero?"

"Yes. I've never seen such bravery. The British man's attack had eviscerated him; technically, he was already dead. Any other samurai would have fallen. But him… he stayed standing for another few minutes, sustained by a supernatural willpower. He beat the English demon in a duel and forged a path through the Imperial forces, all alone, to get you out of the melee. He would have crawled if necessary."

"That's impossible," murmured Atsuko. "He never protected me. Even when I was in danger, he didn't care."

"Believe what you will, but during his final moments, he thought only of you, he fought only for you—and he died for you."

Atsuko bowed her head. It was difficult to reconcile what the samurai said with the image she had in her head of her brother. But he seemed wholly sincere, and what reason would he have to lie, anyway?

Ibuka had found his courage right at the end of his life. Did one act of bravery make up for a lifetime of cowardice?

The tears streaming down her face were response enough.

"Why did you save me?" she eventually asked. "You told me we were even."

"Come now, the world would be a sadder place without a woman who can jump from a castle window and go up against the terrible Lloyd with no hesitation," joked the samurai.

"For all the good it did me..." Atsuko grimaced. "And that's not an answer."

"That's true," admitted Masajiro, smiling. "But my other reply can wait a while. This isn't really the time."

Atsuko reclined, her arms crossed. Night was falling and the stars were beginning to appear in the sky. Her stomach was torturing her, but she felt a little more at peace, for the first time in a long time.

"Don't make me be disagreeable and give me the real reason this instant. Or you know I'll have to get up and stab you in the night."

"An admirable character trait," replied Masajiro. "Which brings me to the point."

Atsuko closed her eyes, strongly hoping it wasn't what she thought. What other reason could he have for saving her, except love? She too had felt a strong connection between them at their first meeting, but she was not ready to accept the feelings from another person, and especially not now. In other circumstances, perhaps… but she didn't want to owe him anything. He had saved her life—what would she have to accept in return? To become his wife? His concubine? Or maybe just one intimate night in this clearing? Was that the price for being saved? Was she yet again reduced to the conditions of her gender?

"Would you agree to join the Brotherhood?"

"I don't know if I—" began Atsuko, before opening her eyes. "I mean—*what*?"

"Takeko informed us of your training a while ago. According to her, you're a very promising recruit—with morals, but that's not necessarily a bad thing. And your infiltration of the camp was absolutely perfect."

"You saw me infiltrate the camp?"

"The mission was a particularly difficult one for a novice," explained Masajiro. "Takeko asked if I could keep an eye on you. Which, of course, allowed me to find you very easily because I knew where you'd exit the castle. You see, nothing magic in it."

Atsuko replayed all the scenes in her head until all the pieces of the puzzle finally fell into place.

"You're an Assassin, too."

"Well done. My real name is Matsuo and I work for Captain Brunet."

"But you travel with the Emperor's army!"

"We wouldn't be very good spies if we couldn't infiltrate the enemy camp, right?"

"But… you tried to steal the Masamune with the others! Takeko told me the Assassins' role was to protect it!"

He gave her an even wider smile.

"I knew you were smart. Takeko was, too. I was an insurance policy, of a sort—if things went badly and Lloyd got his hands on the Masamune, I could track its location. And what better way to gain a Templar's trust than fighting Assassins by his side?"

"A Templa-what?"

Masajiro shrugged.

"We'll have time to explain all that later, if you wish to join our ranks. And I can tell you that my superiors will welcome you with open arms when I show them this."

He withdrew the sword from his shirt and Atsuko's eyes gleamed.

"The Masamune!"

"More precisely, Musashi's sword. I was going to wait a while to make you this offer, but you're the one who insisted. So here it is: would you like to join the Brotherhood of Assassins?"

The teenager took a moment to think. The pain in her stomach worsened into a heavy suffering that ached with the absence of her brother.

"Takeko said that you're fighting for free will and that you challenge existing regimes. Does that mean you're the enemies of the Emperor?"

"Most certainly."

"The same Emperor that killed my brother and Takeko?"

"In a far-removed way, yes, the very same."

Atsuko studied the katana's blade. She saw her reflection in the moonlight, the face of a sixteen-year-old teenager with short hair and eyes puffy from crying. A girl who'd won several duels, survived several battles, infiltrated an enemy camp and almost poisoned a well. No—not a teenager, not a girl.

A woman.

But she saw something else in the reflection, too. A face at her side, sweet and stern all at once, a face that had been at her side since birth. She would never forget Ibuka. If he had been capable of change, if he had managed to break free of his fear… then she too could change.

"I am yours," she said.

And she heard a whispering from the sword, the awakening of a samurai who'd been dead for centuries, who had finally found his successor.

Jules Brunet graciously accepted the cup of tea offered to him by consul Parkes.

"Congratulations," he admitted. "You won this battle. But rest assured, some day we will win the war."

"I don't know what war you're talking about," said the British man in surprise. "After all, our countries are at peace."

"Of course," Brunet replied. "Of course."

He sipped his tea, though it was too hot and had been made too quickly—the English pretended to be experts in the art—but the Frenchman was used to the Japanese ceremonies.

"However, the Emperor has complete power," Brunet murmured. "He will ascend to the throne, and it will be the start of a new era. An era without the samurai, the daimyos, and without valor."

"A peaceful era, with a strong state and flourishing economy," corrected Parkes. "And plus, to inaugurate this new age, the Emperor will change his name."

"Oh? What will he be called now?"

"Meiji, I believe."

Characters

Shiba Atsuko: a young Japanese girl, aged 16, from Aizu, sister of Ibuka. She aspired to a life of liberty, and the way of the samurai.

Shiba Ibuka: a young Japanese boy, aged 17, from Aizu. Older brother of Atsuko, he was extremely skilled in combat and destined to have a fine career as a samurai.

Shiba Tanomo: the father of Atsuko and Ibuka. Participated in the Boshin war at his son's side.

Nakano Takeko: a young Japanese woman, aged 21, an expert in wielding the naginata and the only female samurai in the Aizu domain. She participated in the Boshin war and led a female combat unit under daimyo Katamori.

Matsuo: a ronin and agent of Jules Brunet in service of the Brotherhood.

HARRY PARKES: a diplomat and the British consul in Japan, based in Edo from 1865 to 1883.

WILLIAM LLOYD: the right hand of Harry Parkes, a skilled swordsman and a member of the Order of the Templars.

EMPEROR MUTSUHITO: the Emperor best known under the name of Meiji was the 122nd emperor of Japan, from 1867 to 1912. His name also indicates the era of his reign, named the Meiji era, which ended the age of Edo and the feudal system in Japan after the Boshin war.

TOKUGAWA YOSHINOBU: the last Shogun of the Tokugawa shogunate and feudal Japan. He abdicated his power to the Emperor in 1867, plunging Japan into a new era: one without samurai.

JULES BRUNET: the general of the French division sent to Japan to support Shogun Tokugawa and his army of samurai. French contact in Japan for the Brotherhood of Assassins.

MATSUDAIRA KATAMORI: a samurai and ninth daimyo of the Aizu domain.

MIYAMOTO MUSASHI: an emblematic figure of Japan from the sixth century. He was a master of bushi, a painter, philosopher, and the most famous swordsman in the country.